CAKE IT TO HEART

RAISED AND GLAZED COZY MYSTERIES,
BOOK 14

EMMA AINSLEY

SUMMER PRESCOTT BOOKS PUBLISHING

CHAPTER ONE

"Something is poking me hard in my ribs," Orson Hawley grumbled. He shifted in his place. An elderly woman on a stool in front of him swatted at his legs.

"Mr. Hawley, need I remind you of the important role you are fulfilling during this wedding? You are essentially the father-of-the-bride," she scolded. "So, please, behave like it."

"Your pins are sticking through and piercing my skin," Orson complained.

"Yes, as pins are known to do," she said. "This is why one doesn't seek out a fitting for the mere amusement of it."

"I have some coffee for you, Mrs. Pennyworth," Maggie Sharpe called out from her kitchen. She'd decided to host the fitting in the living room of her small cottage home. Maggie, the owner of Dogwood Donuts, knew the dining room of her business was not the place for such things but she still wanted to make sure everyone was comfortable.

Myra Sawyer, the bride-to-be, rented a room from the grumpy older man being poked by pins, but the air conditioning unit in their old house had gone on the fritz again so Maggie had offered up her own home. She knew there was no way everyone would be able to pile into a house with no cool air and manage not to start a fight.

"I will take that cup," Kathleen Pennyworth announced. "This friend of yours is a bit of a character," she said to Maggie when they were alone in the kitchen.

"That's why we love him," Maggie said, hoping to ease the older woman's tension. Orson's was the last of the fittings needed for the big event. The bride had her dress hanging neatly in her closet. The groom's suit was pressed and waiting at the home of the Chief of Police, his boss, and best man. Brooks Macklin was a lucky young man in Maggie's eyes, and not just because he was marrying her dear young friend and employee, Myra.

Maggie's affections for Brett Mission had played on her mind since the night Myra had popped the question to Orson, asking him to escort her down the aisle. Of course, in her case, the aisle would be the walkway down the middle of the barn on Ruby Cobbs' property between square hay bales stacked at the ends of the rows of chairs for the few dozen guests who would be in attendance. Ruby, Maggie's business partner, and best friend had not only offered her quaint farm as a setting for the wedding but had also offered her skills as a trained chef to help make the reception unforgettable.

"I suppose I better return to my patient," Mrs. Pennyworth laughed. She carried her coffee cup with her and headed back into the living room.

Immediately, Maggie heard Orson begin to grumble again. Mrs. Pennyworth made clucking sounds with her tongue. "I did a fitting out at the Dogwood House with one Gretchen LeClair," she said casually. "It would be a shame for her date not to look as sharp as she will in her dress. And oh, that dress. What a work of art!"

"You did a fitting on Gretchen?" Orson asked quietly.

"I did, and she was quite talkative about her excitement for the event and her date," Mrs. Penny-worth continued. "I truly hope that her date is as elegant as she will be for the wedding."

Orson harrumphed and stood up a little taller on the stool while the dressmaker tucked a few more pins for hems in his pants. She instructed for him to step down next, and then checked over the waistband without a single complaint uttered. Maggie was glad she wasn't in the room with them. She would have had an impossible time attempting to control her facial expressions. Orson might be thankful Myra had asked him to walk her down the aisle, but he wasn't thrilled that would result in Myra moving out of his house. His girlfriend, Gretchen, had offered him a room at her bed and breakfast, the Dogwood House, but the mere idea of that had Orson's emotions in tangles.

"I taught junior high boys for many years before I retired to live out my dreams as a seamstress," she whispered to Maggie later in the kitchen. "Young or old. They're all pretty much the same." With a wink, she left and promised the alterations would be ready in no time at all.

"I'm so glad that's over," Orson announced when he emerged from her bathroom a moment later.

"What's going on over at your house? With the air conditioning, I mean?" Maggie asked.

Orson shrugged. "I've already had the repairman out to take a look at it," he said. "I'm just going to get by with it for now. The old unit is about to give up the ghost is all, and there isn't much that can be done for it this time, short of replacing the entire thing."

"Do you need..."

"No, I don't need anything right now," he said, smiling for once. "I have a few fans running in essential places and it's not too unbearable outside yet, anyway. Myra will be moving out before I know it, and after that I'll decide whether or not I want to fix things or move on from the house entirely."

"You mean to Gretchen's?" She winked.

"No, I do not mean to Gretchen's," he said with finality in his voice.

Maggie felt her heart sink. She hadn't considered the possibility of Orson moving away. "But where would you go? That's your home, for better or for worse," she said.

Orson nodded. "And you might remember much of that has been for the worst," he said. In the beginning, the realtor who sold him the house failed to disclose many of its problems, forcing him to spend money he didn't have in order to make it more livable. Maggie was unsure how much of his continuing to work at the donut shop still had to do with the maintenance of those issues. And Myra moving out would mean the loss of some rental income, too.

"But where would you live?" Maggie asked again. The small town of Dogwood Mountain offered few choices for senior citizens on a fixed income.

"Joplin, I guess." Orson smiled again, this time through sad eyes. Maggie felt her heart lurch again.

"No, no." Orson waved off her concern. "Right now, we're focused on getting that girl of ours married off to that young man of hers."

"Right," Maggie said. She turned away from him and swiped a tear from her eye. "Let's get these plates packed up and out to the farm so we can cross that off of the to-do list."

Orson nodded and picked up the first small box. Maggie had learned not to insist on picking up heavy things when he was around. He simply wouldn't allow it. Her strategy was to pack heavy things in smaller packages where she could. The plates she had were on loan from her friend Flo Johnson, who had them leftover from her diner in a nearby town. Now, Flo operated a food truck out of the donut shop parking lot and served her diner food on disposable plates, but she was more than happy to share what she had with her new friends.

They loaded the boxes into the back of Maggie's car and just as she shut the trunk, Jake Jenkins,

Maggie's garage tenant and newest employee, emerged from behind them.

"What are you up to this evening?" she asked the younger man. In her mind, he was still the frightened, homeless boy who came to town from his home up the mountain with his relatives. But he had grown up a bit in the recent months, working both for her at the donut shop and Flo at the food truck.

"I'm doing some maintenance work on Flo's house," he said. "She needs a bird's nest cleaned out of the chimney flue."

"Have fun with that," Maggie said. "I'm off to Ruby's with these plates for the wedding. Orson might be hanging around a bit if you get lonely when you come back from Flo's."

Jake nodded and headed off. She made an excuse for Orson to hang around her house for a little while. She told him she wasn't sure how to change the filters on her own air conditioning unit. She also mentioned a noise in the dryer, a loss of water pressure only in the shower, and anything else she could come up with to keep him there while his house struggled to remain at a decent temperature.

Anything for Orson, the curmudgeon that he was deserved everything good in this world.

CHAPTER TWO

Maggie backed her car into Ruby's driveway. She popped her trunk and waved to her friend when she emerged from the farmhouse. A load of hay was visible inside of the large barn that wasn't too far away from where she stood.

"Looking good over there," Maggie said to her best friend. Somehow, it looked as though the wood on the outside of the barn gleamed in sunlight.

"I just had it power washed if you can believe that," Ruby said. "Turns out you can power wash the outside of a barn without ruining the wood. At least, that's what the guy I hired said when he was finished."

"Whatever he did, it looks great." Maggie picked

up a box with ease and headed inside the back of the farmhouse.

"How did the fitting go for Orson?"

Maggie laughed. "About like you would expect," she said. "Mrs. Pennyworth brought out the big guns.

She mentioned Miss Gretchen LeClair and how fetching she will look for the wedding."

"Aha," Ruby said. "And I bet Orson clammed right up after that."

"He uttered nary a word of complaint after that," Maggie said with a grin. "He didn't even make note of the smaller sizes of the boxes I got for packing these dishes."

"That's a miracle in itself," Ruby said as she picked up a box of her own. They placed them on the freezer in the mudroom at the back of the farmhouse. "I'm a little sad that Myra wouldn't let us make her wedding cake, though."

"You mean that she wouldn't let you make the wedding cake," Maggie said. "I think she expects a stack of donuts or scones from me. I'm not a cake maker."

"Yeah, I guess it's just as well." Ruby shrugged. "I'm sure I have more than enough to do to keep me busy."

Maggie's eyes widened as she nodded her head.

"Gee, you think? You're taking on a momentous task and you're doing it all alone, basically."

"Oh, I have help coming," Ruby said. "My editor friend is sending down her niece and a friend to help me out."

"That sounds like it will be wonderful. Are these girls experienced?"

"Actually, I think it's the niece and a guy, but yeah. They're both culinary students and this counts as some sort of informal internship I guess," Ruby said.

Maggie helped her pull the plates out of the box and arrange them in stacks for the dishwasher. The plan was to wash them and then place them in a spare cabinet. Once the boxes were empty, Ruby invited Maggie to walk out into the pasture to look at the progression of the decorations.

The warm air hit them hard when they walked back outside. Maggie pulled her sleeves up as they walked. "I can't believe how warm it is already. I hope we have a cooler day for the wedding."

"I'm just hopeful for no rain," Ruby said.

"Hush. Bite your tongue." Maggie chuckled. "Really, though, even if it does rain, you've created something amazing in the barn that will be perfect no matter the weather."

Maggie gasped. They walked through the large doors that led into the barn. The air was even warmer inside. Even with the doors on the far end open to accommodate the stacks of hay, the inside of the barn didn't have much of a cross breeze.

Ruby flipped a switch at one end. The middle of the floor was immediately illuminated by strings of soft light that lined the walls. The lights encircled a hand-built trellis at the front where the nuptials would take place. Maggie noted the lace-on-burlap decorations, Mason jars fitted with lights, and reclaimed wood tables.

"Who did all of this?" Maggie asked, pointing at the newly made tables.

"Brooks did this," Ruby said. "Along with the help of his best man, of course."

"Really? Brett helped him? He didn't tell me."

"Really. Apparently, the police chief is quite handy." Ruby grinned.

"I'll have to keep that in mind the next time I need something done around my house." Maggie laughed.

"I think you'd be wise to reconsider. Orson would have your head."

"Fair point. I don't want to do anything that might upset him." Maggie paused and looked down at her feet for a moment before letting out a sigh. "I think he might be considering moving away."

"Wait, what? You're talking about Orson? I know he's against moving into the bed and breakfast with Gretchen but what do you mean moving away? He's not seriously that upset about Myra moving out, is he?"

"I'm not sure. I thought he had come around and was happy for her but he's a hard man to read. All I know is that I don't want to give him any reason on my end to think moving out of Dogwood Mountain is a good idea." Maggie finally looked up with another tear in her eye.

A noise outside saved them from having to over-think about Orson. They could hear the sound of tires crunching over gravel, and quite fast. Ruby glanced at Maggie and headed for the open door to see who had arrived in such a hurry.

"That's Myra," she announced. "I wonder if something is wrong."

Maggie said nothing but followed her outside toward the house. Myra was parked directly behind her car. She was on the phone with someone. They could hear raised voices through the car's speakers. What was being said, they could not understand. But Maggie was sure the other speaker was a woman. She sighed a little in relief that the engaged couple was not fighting, at least not that they knew about.

As they walked a little closer, they could hear the engine running and the voices rising. Myra beat the steering wheel as she spoke. The voice on the other end was openly hostile. Myra asked something about a deposit. She tried not to listen, but it was difficult to ignore the words coming from the speakers.

All at once, the engine roared and the car lurched forward. Maggie watched helplessly as Myra's car crashed into her bumper. She stopped walking and blinked in disbelief. Ruby stopped too and grabbed her arm. "Oh, no," she said. "Oh, Maggie. I'm so sorry. I'm sure she didn't mean to do that." Since Myra had come into their lives, Ruby had been very protective of the younger woman.

"I can't believe that just happened," Maggie said, still in disbelief.

"Listen," Ruby said. She turned to face her. "I'll take care of the repairs. Whatever it takes. I know Myra is going to feel awful. They have scraped and saved up for their honeymoon and I don't want them to have to give that up."

Maggie frowned at her friend. "I don't want her to, either. You're not the only one who loves those kids. Besides," she said, feeling a little better. "We're both insured. That's what insurance is for, after all."

The voice on the other end of Myra's phone was screaming into the speakers. Myra ended the phone call, pulled her car back from where it was pressed against the back of Maggie's, and shut the engine off. She got out of the car with her hand over her mouth.

"Oh, I am so, so sorry," she said. With her car pulled back, Maggie got a better look at the damage. The car had hit more than just her bumper. The entire back end of the car had caved in. "I have money. We have money. I promise we will get your car back to new. Oh, my gosh. I can't believe I just did that."

Myra stopped a few feet from them and crumbled forward in a fit of tears. She sobbed and sobbed. Maggie felt her heart breaking for the girl. Ruby cast her a knowing look.

"Hey, hey," Ruby said when she reached Myra. She wrapped her arms around the younger woman and let her sob on her shoulder for a long moment.

"Okay, okay," Maggie said, breaking in between them. "Enough of this." Myra pulled back, closed her eyes, and inhaled deeply, and then opened her eyes to face Maggie.

"Let's take a better look at the damage," Maggie said. She gripped the girl by her shoulders and turned her around to face the cars. "Do you see that? This is why we both pay insurance premiums. Okay? It's going to be alright, Myra."

"She's right, hon," Ruby said. "Get your insurance information and give it to Maggie. She'll call her agent and things will get worked out."

"That's exactly right," Maggie said. She waited while Myra retrieved her insurance card from her glove box. "Now, why don't we take a moment and head inside so you can tell us what all that yelling was about," Maggie suggested. "We can call our insurance companies after that. We want to make sure you are okay first."

With that, fresh tears started to flow.

CHAPTER THREE

An hour later, Maggie's car was towed out of the driveway at her agent's insistence. "I don't think it was necessary," she'd complained to Ruby and Myra.

"I feel so bad," Myra said again. "Now you're without a vehicle and, of course, mine doesn't even look that bad."

"No, she isn't," Ruby said with a grin. "Now, she gets to drive Beulah for however long it takes for her to get her car back."

"Oh, no," Maggie said in mock surprise. "Not Beastly Beulah!" Beulah was the name given to the 1980s-era flatbed farm truck Ruby had recently added to the farm. The truck was difficult to start and in need of a better muffler.

"Now I'm even more sorry," Myra's voice cracked.

"Young lady," Maggie said in her best mom voice. "If you don't stop apologizing, I'm going to make you clean out every deep fryer in the donut shop and the food truck with a toothbrush."

Myra's eyes widened for a moment. "Okay, message received," she said. "This week has been so stressful. I thought a simple wedding meant less anxiety."

"Are you ready to tell us what happened with the lady on the phone?" Ruby asked. When the women had first arrived in the house, Myra had done her very best to avoid the topic. She insisted they call their insurance companies before anything else and then they'd spent almost a half-hour discussing a new recipe for a brioche donut.

Myra nodded and sighed. "I was talking to the baker from Joplin," she said. "Now, I know what you two said about making the wedding cake, but this lady was highly recommended and reasonable. That is, until this morning. She was supposed to meet up with me with cake samples, but she never showed. When I called her, she just started screaming at me that I was being a bridezilla."

"Did she ever tell you why she was a no-show?"

Ruby asked. She adored Myra, but sometimes the younger woman could forget that other people had last-minute emergencies, too.

Myra shook her head. "She basically blamed me for setting the appointment in the first place. Like, somehow I was inconveniencing her by giving her my business. I know this is sort of last minute, but she didn't need to agree to meet with me at all if it was a problem."

"That sounds very unprofessional," Ruby said.

"You can say that again," Maggie agreed. "What are you going to do now?"

Myra shrugged. "I'm not sure yet. I got a call from Daisy McNorris, the baker's assistant, just as I ended the call with my insurance agent. She said she would meet me at the donut shop tomorrow around eleven with samples." She eyed Maggie. "I know you probably don't want it to happen there, but I had to take what I could get. I hope it's okay."

"It's perfectly fine," Maggie said with an encouraging smile. "Everything is going to be okay."

"I'm not so sure," Myra said, still frowning. "Daisy is apparently Wanda's ex-assistant. She just quit working for her and is starting out on her own."

"And you said yes to meeting her?" Maggie asked.

"Well, technically, Daisy didn't tell me she quit, it was Wanda," Myra tried to rationalize.

Ruby shook her head. "You ought to be careful. It sounds to me like this Daisy woman isn't being truthful. I'd hate to think that she was offering to bring you samples under the guise that she's still working for Wanda."

"Well, like I said, I have to take what I can get. If Wanda doesn't want my business, I'll just have to hope that Daisy is as good of a baker as her ex-boss." Myra shrugged half-heartedly. "But there's just one other problem. Daisy said she's going to need a deposit and Wanda very openly refused to give me mine back. And if you ask me, that's just as bad as whatever Daisy is trying to do. All I want is a wedding cake and I don't care what personal mess they have going on. That's none of my business."

"She is refusing to give you back your deposit even though she's the one who flaked on your meeting?"

Ruby asked. "And you're sure she wasn't planning on rescheduling?"

"I'm sure. It was pretty obvious by all the yelling that she no longer wants to work with me," Myra said sarcastically.

"Right." Ruby nodded. "Sorry."

"She said she was firing me as her client and that the wording of our contract says that she can end the contract at any moment and for any reason and still keep my deposit!" Fresh tears rolled down her cheeks.

"If that's the case, there isn't much you can do," Ruby said. "But don't worry about the deposit."

"She's right," Maggie said. "If you don't mind me asking, how much did you pay Wanda, and what is Daisy asking for?

"Half up front, plus another hundred dollars because it's so last minute, and another hundred because she is taking over for Wanda Reiss," Myra said.

"That's practically highway robbery," Maggie said.

"And awfully suspicious," Ruby muttered.

"It is, but it's what I need to do right now," Myra said.

Maggie stood up and excused herself to the bathroom. Once she was there, she texted Orson with instructions to pull several hundred dollars in cash from the safe she kept in her office at the donut shop. The shop was closed for the day, but she knew Orson wouldn't mind stopping in to help.

"The deposit is ready and waiting for you when

you come into work first thing in the morning," she announced when she returned to the living room.

Myra opened her mouth to protest but was immediately cut off by Ruby.

"Remember her threat about the toothbrush and the deep fryers," she said. "I'd take her at her word."

Myra said nothing else. She got up from her seat and enveloped Maggie in a crushing hug.

Ruby treated the pair to an impromptu meal of garlic butter pork chops and cheddar bacon twice baked potatoes. They talked and enjoyed each other's company but avoided any topics related to the wedding or Orson mentioning moving away. The last thing Myra needed was the weight of that on her shoulders.

As she was getting ready to leave, Maggie tapped Myra on her shoulder. "You are not allowed to get so stressed out and worried, okay?"

"I'll do my best," Myra said with doubt in her eyes.

"Listen," Maggie said. "If you start to get freaked out over something, I want you to come and find me. You and I will stop whatever we're doing and sit down and work it out. Got it?"

Myra nodded. "I'm really happy, despite all of this stuff going on around me," she said. "I never thought I would meet someone as wonderful as Brooks, and so soon after what happened to me before."

"You deserve to be happy, and weddings should be filled with joy, not so much stress," Maggie said. "My marriage didn't turn out the way I thought it would, but I still have beautiful memories of my wedding.

And then of course the memories were even sweeter after the birth of my son."

"How are Bradley and little Wyatt?"

Maggie smiled at the mention of her son and grandson. "Still thriving," she said. "I have a feeling Bradley is a lot happier these days. Wyatt has finally begun to sleep through the night again. He's been teething. And boy, do I know all about that. Bradley has no qualms about calling his mother in the middle of the night when he has a question about the baby."

"Like you mind that," Ruby teased. "You know you love it."

"I'll remember that when he calls me next time. I might have to redirect his question to Aunt Ruby," Maggie said rolling her eyes.

"What makes you think he's never called me with a question?"

Maggie was taken off guard. "Bradley has called you? In the middle of the night?"

"Well, not in the middle of the night," Ruby said. "But he has called me before with an emergency culinary question. Especially when he made dinner for a young woman from the base."

"Wait, wait, what are you talking about? I didn't hear about this," Maggie said. Myra was seated on the couch covering her mouth with a throw pillow to hide her fit of giggles at their antics.

"That's because he didn't want you to hear about it," Ruby said. "That's why I'm Aunt Ruby. I can keep secrets."

"But can you?" Maggie said. "What happened with this girl? Are they dating?"

Ruby shook her head." Nothing happened. She canceled on him with a text message in the middle of his trip to the commissary," she said. "I know that because he was calling to ask me about curry paste versus curry powder. Believe me, if more had happened with her, you would have known."

"That's good to know, at least," Maggie said. She elbowed Ruby lightly in the ribs. "Traitor."

"I'm not a traitor," Ruby said. "Just a good aunt."

"He's lucky to have you both. We all are." Myra

stood and stretched her arms over her head. "I'm going to head home," she announced. "If the air isn't working too well, I would like to be the one to figure it out instead of Orson. I'm sure he's still out running errands or at Gretchen's. Anything not to be in that house alone."

"I wish he would let us help him," Maggie said.

"He deserves his dignity," Ruby said. "Although I definitely agree with you." She left the room for a moment and returned with the keys to Beulah. "Speaking of dignity, be sure to keep one foot on the gas when you go around corners. The clutch is a little iffy."

"Thanks, I think," Maggie said. She walked out of the door ahead of Myra.

"Hang on," Myra said when she stepped outside. "I just got a text message from Wanda Reiss."

"Oh, boy," Ruby groaned. "What could she possibly want?"

"She said she wants to meet with me at six tomorrow morning," Myra said. "I don't know what I should do."

"Where does she want to meet you?" Maggie asked.

"She said she'll come to the donut shop," Myra said.

"Did she say that she'll meet you with samples or anything?" Maggie asked.

Myra shook her head. "No, but she did mention talking about my deposit."

"Then it sounds like good news." Maggie smiled. "Maybe everything will work out after all."

"I'm not so sure," Ruby said. "Call me Negative Nancy, but it sounds to me like these two are playing some sort of game with you."

"I said it once, and I'll say it twelve more times if I have to. I don't care one bit about whatever drama they have going on. If Wanda says she'll make my cake, I'll have plenty of time to cancel my appointment with Daisy. And if I don't like what Wanda has to say, then I'll have Daisy in my back pocket, just in case." Myra forced a smile. "I think this will work out one way or another. It has to."

CHAPTER FOUR

Maggie shivered while she tried to shove her key into the back door lock. The old pickup truck never warmed up between her house and the donut shop. Despite the closeness of the house to the donut shop, Maggie froze in her seat. She couldn't believe how quickly the temperature had changed from the day before.

"At least Myra and Orson weren't too uncomfortable last night," she said to Ruby a few minutes later.

Ruby yawned when she nodded in agreement. She relayed the story of her own morning and a cow that decided to give birth at three in the morning.

"Sometimes I wonder how you handle work here and at the farm at the same time," Maggie said.

"I live for the new flavors we add to the menu,"

Ruby said with an eye-roll. "By the way, you mentioned wanting to try a new latte flavor this morning. I could really use the caffeine right about now."

"Right." Maggie smiled. "You get settled in and I'll go whip one up for you."

"Sounds good," Ruby agreed. "Make it extra hot and with a double shot of espresso if you don't mind. I can't get over how cool it is outside."

Maggie kept her comments about Old Beulah to herself. She was too grateful for the use of it to complain about the heater. Instead, she headed for the front and turned on the espresso machine. She waited while the machine warmed up. When it was ready, she mixed caramel and mocha syrups with a touch of marshmallow into the bottom of two cups. She poured a double shot into Ruby's and decided on a single for herself. After filling the cups with perfectly frothed milk, she went all out and added whipped cream and a drizzle of mocha sauce to the tops of each latte.

"Tell me what you think," she said when she handed the extra-hot, extra-caffeinated beverage over to Ruby. After a moment, her eyes widened. "Oh, my gosh," she said. "Does this have marshmallow in it?"

"And caramel and mocha, too," Maggie said. "I thought this would pair nicely with my other surprise this morning. I've added marshmallow syrup to the mocha frosting for the chocolate-filled donuts."

"Will you drizzle caramel over the top?"

"As if there was another option." Maggie winked.

"Sounds absolutely perfect."

"Good morning," Myra called out from the back door a moment later. "Oh, it's nice and warm in here."

"Funny to hear you say that after all the trouble with the air conditioning at your house," Maggie said.

Myra nodded. "It was great to sleep well last night. I think we both needed it more than we knew. Orson said he'll be in around eight. I guess he had something to take care of this morning."

"Good," Maggie said, trying not to let her mind wander to what Orson could be doing. "You're supposed to meet with Wanda here at six, right?"

"No, now she wants to meet me at a gas station in Hunter Springs," Myra said. "If that isn't okay, I'll just tell her I can't. I know I have a job to do here and with Orson coming in later today, I totally understand if you don't want me to."

"Why does she want to meet you so far away?" Ruby asked, ignoring the rest.

Myra shrugged. "Something about how far she has to come from Joplin. I almost don't think it's worth it to meet with her, but if she gives me at least part of my deposit back, it might be worth it. I've already come to terms with the fact that she's likely not going to do the cake since she wants to meet at a gas station, but if I can get a little money back and keep my meeting with Daisy, then I'll be okay."

Ruby rubbed her temples and took a deep breath in. "You should probably just forget about it and leave a bad review for her business if you feel like you have to do something."

"And I think you ought to get yourself some coffee and a quick breakfast if you're going to drive all that way," Maggie said. "I agree it's probably better to just forget about Wanda, but I understand wanting to recoup some of your hard-earned money."

"What about work?" Myra asked, shooting a look of thanks at Maggie. "I probably won't be back until after seven."

"Jake is on his way in," Maggie announced.

"You're sure?" Myra asked again.

"Go." Maggie pointed to the door. "Take a couple of donuts with you and grab a coffee on the way out."

"I really hope things go well for her," Ruby said. "I'm worried she is going to get there and deal with more nonsense from this woman."

"I think you're forgetting how badly Myra wants to be independent. She appreciates our help, and we know that, but it's important to her that she doesn't need to rely on us for everything. She wants to prove she can handle things on her own and that might mean she needs to deal with an annoying business owner who isn't all that great at business."

"Yeah," Ruby conceded.

Maggie set the last of the new 'caramocello' donuts on the top row of the display case. She was always a bit worried about putting out something new, however, the placement on the top row was almost better advertisement than taking out an ad in the paper.

"Those look amazing," Jake said as he tied an apron around his waist. He seldom commented about the pastries at the donut shop, despite how many he managed to eat. Maggie smiled and removed two from the case and placed them on a sheet of waxed paper for him.

"Tell me what you think," she said quietly. "But if you don't like them, tell me back in the kitchen."

"Got it," Jake whispered back. Maggie smiled at the rare hint at Jake's personality.

The first rush of customers filled the dining room. Maggie busied herself with their orders while Ruby handled the kitchen. Jake ran in between and helped as much as he could. When the line thinned about an hour later, Maggie rushed back into the kitchen for a sip of coffee and a chance to get off of her feet.

"Remind me to tell Myra how valuable she is," she said to Ruby. "It's so different not having her here to help."

"Trust me, I have the same message for her myself," Ruby said. "How is it that she can manage the customers out front and help us back here? Good grief, I hope she doesn't have any plans to work anywhere else."

"Have you heard something?" Maggie chewed on the thought for a moment. "You would tell me if she had said anything, wouldn't you?"

Ruby nodded. "Of course, I would, but you know that already. And while she hasn't said anything, I kind of feel like there is something she might be hiding."

"What makes you think that?" Maggie asked. She was a little surprised to see the animation in Ruby's typically stoic face.

"Because I asked her all about their plans for the future and what she's going to do when they get back from their honeymoon, and she just tells me that they are working on it," Ruby said.

"Working on what?" Maggie asked.

"That's the whole thing," Ruby whispered. "I

don't know what she means. I asked her to elaborate but she's being a little bit evasive. You know Myra. She's normally an open book with me."

"She is," Maggie agreed. "By the way, have you heard anything from her since she left? Do you know if Wanda was a no-show again?"

"I haven't heard anything, no," Ruby said, a worried look creeping onto her face.

"Maggie? Someone out here is asking for Myra," Jake said a second later. He held the swinging door between the dining room and kitchen open for her. Maggie glanced at Ruby on her way out. She hoped that the visit from whoever was asking for Myra did not mean more complications in the wedding plans.

"Can I help you?" she asked the woman waiting on the other side of the counter.

"Are you Myra? You seem a little old to be the bride-to-be," the woman said with a scrunched nose. She glared at Maggie over the top of her wire-rimmed glasses.

Through tight lips, Maggie replied as kindly as she was able, "I'm not Myra, but I am the owner of this establishment and a close friend. Myra isn't here right at the moment. How can I help you?"

"I was supposed to meet her here this morning to discuss her wedding cake," she said. She raised the plastic case in her hand up to the counter. "I have samples for her to try. Are you seriously telling me that she isn't here?"

Maggie stared at the woman for a moment. "Are you Daisy or Wanda?"

"Daisy," she said, clearly offended. "I am no longer associated with Wanda Reiss or her bakery."

"Okay, well, Myra was under the impression that you were supposed to meet with her at eleven o'clock," Maggie said. "She went to meet with Wanda to discuss her deposit."

"Oh, dear," Daisy said. "Maybe I got my times wrong. Is it possible for me to sit and wait for her?" Her initial crusty demeanor had softened.

"Of course," Maggie agreed. "Can I get you a cup of coffee, on the house?"

"Oh, that would be lovely," Daisy said. She accepted the cup and settled into a booth on the far end of the counter.

Maggie returned to the kitchen and took a seat back on her stool.

"What's that face about?" Ruby asked. "You look absolutely bewildered."

"Do you think all bakers have trouble telling time?"

"What are we late for?" Ruby asked.

"Not us," Maggie said. "That lady Myra was supposed to meet at eleven to sample wedding cake flavors is sitting right out there in a booth with a free cup of coffee waiting for Myra to return from her meeting with the first wedding cake baker who has given more run around than anyone I have ever heard of!"

"Good grief," Ruby said. She plucked her phone off of the shelf above the prep table. "I'm going to call Myra and let her know."

Before she could dial her number, Myra pushed the back door open with gusto. "Some people," she said. Her face was flushed red.

"What happened to you?" Maggie gasped.

Myra sat her bag down hard on the floor. She unwound the scarf from her neck and shucked off her coat. "I drove all the way down the highway to Hunter Springs and that woman was a no-show, again!"

"Are you serious? She stood you up again?"

"Without a phone call. She won't return my text messages! I am so mad I could spit!" Myra slumped down onto a stool outside the storeroom.

"Not to stir up more frustration, but that other baker is out there waiting for you right now," Maggie said.

"What?" Myra flopped her arms over her head, resembling a frustrated three-year-old. Maggie had to turn her head to hold in her laughter. "Are you just kidding around with me?"

Maggie shook her head slowly. "No, Myra. She showed up just a few minutes ago asking for you," she said.

"Oh, I can't even handle this right now. I'm this close to just serving donuts at this wedding," she said, pinching her fingers together. "I'll be back as soon as I'm done talking with her and I'll stay late to help clean up, too. I'm so sorry for causing such chaos."

CHAPTER FIVE

Maggie and Ruby took turns peeking through the swinging door at Myra and Daisy. Maggie reported the sampling of the cakes. Ruby looked next and reported an apparent agreement on a flavor, although she wasn't sure which one Myra had picked.

Almost an hour later, Myra returned to the kitchen smiling from ear to ear. "I have a cake!" she sang and danced around in a circle.

"What flavor did you go with?" Maggie asked.

"Chocolate raspberry cream." Myra beamed. "That's for the tiered wedding cake. Just a small, basic cake. She's also making two half-sheet cakes. One will be the same flavor, and the other one will be vintage vanilla."

"What is vintage vanilla?" Maggie asked.

"It's just vanilla," Ruby said. "Vintage means it's the old flavor everyone already knows and loves and will be just fine with in case they have an issue with the other flavor."

"That's just about what Daisy said." Myra nodded.

"Did she offer any sort of reason why she was so early this morning?" Maggie asked, unable to contain her curiosity.

Myra nodded. "She blames Wanda's business partner, John Michael. He's making things tough on her because she decided to up and quit and now she is competition for the two of them."

"You know what?" Ruby cut in. "Now that you've got the cake ordered, you can just let the rest of this go."

"You're right." Myra grinned. "I suppose the best thing I can do is forget the name Wanda Reiss and anything else to do with her."

"That's right. Now you can be free to dream about your honeymoon," Maggie said.

"Ahhh, yes. Catalina Island," Myra said slowly. "Off the coast of California, and I can't wait to be there."

"Sounds fantastic," Jake said as he popped back out of the kitchen as quickly as he'd come in.

"I still can't believe Brooks picked it. I was good with Branson." Myra placed the tray of cups Jake had handed her into the sink.

"Branson? You have got to be kidding me!" Ruby tossed a towel at her. "You are getting married, not going for a weekend with your friend!"

Myra blushed slightly. "I'm well aware of the fact that this is a once-in-a-lifetime trip," she said. She tossed the towel back at Ruby with a grin.

"What are your plans after the honeymoon?" Maggie asked. She looked over at Ruby, who shook her head slightly when she spoke. "I mean, I assume you plan to continue your job here and Brooks is going to stay on at the Dogwood Mountain Police Department for the time being."

"I don't think Brooks ever intends to leave the police department or this town," Myra said. "Now, if you'll excuse me, I need to go up front and earn the money you so generously pay me."

Myra grabbed a clean apron from the hook on the wall. She tied it around her waist as she walked back out front. The moment the swinging door had slowed down, Maggie sidled up closer to Ruby. "Did you notice how she said Brooks doesn't intend on leaving town but didn't include herself in that statement?"

"Yes, and I can't help but feel like we're the

parents of a teenager with deep, dark secrets." She frowned and leaned in to Maggie.

"I feel more like we're the parents of that brown-nosing kid from Leave it to Beaver."

"Eddie Haskell? The one who was always saying 'Hello, Mr. and Mrs. Cleaver' but you knew he would be the first one to bring a fifth of vodka into Wally's bedroom on a sleepover?" Ruby laughed.

"That would be the one," Maggie said. "Only, I don't know if what we're dealing with is better or worse than a fifth of vodka." She shrugged and returned to her cinnamon roll dough. While the dough rested and raised for the first time, Ruby was busy at the prep table with her latest creation, a spicy green salad with chopped seasoned beef, black beans, roasted corn, and salsa. She refused to call it a "taco salad," but Maggie thought it looked exactly like one.

She announced it was time for a short break and headed to the front for a latte. Orson greeted her when she came through the doors. "What are you doing up here?" he asked.

"Why are you so grumpy?" Maggie shot back. "Actually, when did you even get here?"

"Well, I," Orson stuttered, He was rarely called out on his grumpiness. "I don't know why I'm so grumpy. I think I'm just feeling a little lonely these days is all. And I got here a little after eight. I decided to come in through the front to avoid what's happening right now, honestly."

"Why? Do you know something and are you avoiding talking to me about it?" Maggie asked, staring at him.

"What is this, an interrogation?" Orson crossed his arms. "I was late for work and I'm sorry. It won't happen again."

"No, I'm sorry. I'm just feeling a bit paranoid is all. After you told me you might be moving away, I started to worry, and now I can't help but think there is something odd going on with Myra and what her plans are for after the wedding. I thought you might know something."

Orson shook his head. "I have invited them to return and live in my house as long as they want to," he said. "A month ago, they were talking all the time about saving money for a house. And now they say nothing about it. I wonder if the real world zapped their dreams right out of their heads."

"Oh, I hope not," Maggie said. "I mean, we all know the cost of buying a new house is on the rise again."

"What can I get for you? Would you like a coffee?" he asked in a sudden fit of kindness. Either that or it was a clever way to change the subject, which only served to make Maggie even more concerned.

"I came up here for a latte," she said. "But I can get it myself."

"Nonsense," he said and chased her from behind the counter. He quickly whipped her up a caramo-cello latte from the recipe card she'd left by the espresso machine and set it in front of her at her usual booth a few minutes later. "Mind if I join you?"

"Of course not," Maggie said as she looked around the room to make sure all the customers were taken care of. She sipped the latte and closed her eyes. "How is it that you manage to make these lattes ten times better than I can?"

"It's all in the wrist," Orson said. He flipped his hand upward and posed like an artist with a paint-brush in his fingers. Maggie laughed and drank more of the latte.

"I have a secret project I'm working on right now," she said.

"Is that right?" Orson asked. "What mess are you about to drag me into now?"

"Very funny." Maggie rolled her eyes. "I was thinking of making one of those donut trees like we did for Christmas, but instead I'd like to do a wedding theme for the morning of the wedding."

"I think that's a nice idea, but what exactly does a wedding theme look like?" Orson asked.

"To be honest with you, I have no idea, but I've got four separate dishes of buttercream frosting in the cooler right now to experiment with," Maggie said. "I want to do something with the wedding colors, I think. Maybe something with hearts?"

"Hearts, huh? Are you thinking a donut tree, or something with a cinnamon roll dough?"

He drummed his fingers on the table. "What if we can fashion some sort of cherry cordial mold? I know for a fact that both Brooks and Myra love them. Maybe we could shape them into hearts and attach them to the tree for decoration?"

Maggie stared at him with her mouth open. "Orson, that's brilliant. And if we do that, we could do a whole chocolate-cherry theme. So, a donut tree with cherry filling and chocolate icing, and then the heart cherry cordials."

Orson grinned once more. "I can't take the credit. I got the idea from an old winter issue of some foody magazine at Gretchen's. They were giving instructions on making hot chocolate ball molds and I thought it might work for this."

Maggie leaned up and kissed him on the forehead. "That's a million times better than what I had in mind. Partly because I barely had any ideas yet, but still. This is gold!"

Orson blushed slightly and stood. "You finish that latte and I'll get back to work. Later, we can talk more and come up with some final designs and plans."

"I can't wait to see what we come up with!"

Orson grinned and headed back to the kitchen. Maggie sat and enjoyed the second half of her latte. She was still grinning when Brett walked into the donut shop. He spotted her right away and headed over to her booth.

"Hey, there," she said to him when he slid into the seat across from her.

"Hey, yourself." He smiled and held her eyes for a moment. A shadow crossed his face and he looked away.

"Was there something you needed, Brett?" Maggie asked, a little more impatient than she had meant to be. She knew by the look he was giving her that something was wrong.

"I actually came here to ask you a question," he said. "But I got a phone call on the way over here that changes everything. I just don't want you to hate me for it."

"You aren't making any sense. What are you talking about?"

"Trust me," he said. "You're going to think I'm completely crazy in a moment." He gazed at her again. Maggie was struck by the raw sadness in his eyes.

"Why don't you just spit it out, then?" Maggie challenged him.

"You want the honest truth? I was on my way over here hoping to find business a little dull, kind of like it is now," he said. "I was hoping we could spend some time together since it feels like we've been so busy with wedding stuff and work that we haven't gotten much of a chance to enjoy each other's company lately."

"Okay," Maggie said, looking around. "I'm sure I can carve out some time if you let me go in the back to ask Ruby to cover for me."

Brett smiled briefly before his face fell again. "But the Morton County sheriff called me on my way over here and informed me that she had a dead body on her hands. An older woman was found dead in her car just inside the Morton County line. On the north side of the county."

"What does that have to do with Dogwood Mountain? That's less than thirty miles to Joplin," Maggie said. She felt the same sadness threaten her, although she had no idea why just yet.

"The sheriff received an anonymous tip about the woman," he said. "Her name was Wanda Reiss."

"Oh no, no, no." Maggie shook her head before he could get the rest of it out.

"The tipster told her that Wanda Reiss was on her way to meet a young woman here in town, a new bride by the name of Myra, although there was no last name given."

"You've got to be kidding me," Maggie said. She felt the tears forming in her eyes as she spoke.

"I wish I was." He reached for her hands and clutched them in his own. "Brooks already knows. He's probably talking to Myra right now. You may want to keep an eye on her once she finds out. Brooks was very professional about it and took the rest of the day off. But Maggie, the sheriff is on her way here to bring Myra in for questioning."

"This isn't right." She looked up at him. "There are details you don't know. This woman canceled on Myra, and then sent her on a wild goose chase this morning but never showed up."

"I know," he said and squeezed her hands harder.

"I already know all of it. Brooks filled me in on everything. But this is outside my jurisdiction, and in another county altogether. You know as well as I do that me knowing Myra has nothing to hide isn't going to matter one bit."

CHAPTER SIX

"I just finished telling her that everything was going to be alright now that she had the cake figured out," Maggie said after the Morton County Sheriff had come and gone with Myra in the backseat of a police car.

"They said they were questioning her, but I have a feeling someone has already decided it is more than that," Ruby said.

"This stinks," Orson declared. "The entire thing stinks like a hog farm in July and we all know it! First, this woman flakes out on her, keeps her deposit, and then decides to meet up with her anyway. She's a no-show, and then she winds up dead?"

"I think she was a no-show because she was already dead," Maggie pointed out.

"How did she text message Myra about the change in location then?" Orson demanded.

"Those are all good questions," Brett said. He leaned against the wall next to the cooler. "Someone really ought to look into that."

"I'm worried this whole thing looks like a motive for murder," Ruby chimed in. "I don't like this one bit."

Brett nodded his head. "That part deserves some looking into as well," he said.

"Does anyone else find it odd that her former assistant was ready and willing to jump in and take over the business so fast?" Maggie said. "Not to mention her own struggles with getting the time right this morning."

"All of this is so weird," Ruby said. "I mean, I am very sorry that a woman died. But I feel like Myra has just been swept right up into this whole thing."

"I think it would be really good for someone to look into all of these loose pieces," Brett said again. He cleared his throat.

"What are you saying over there?" Orson asked him.

"He said that someone really ought to look into all of this," Jake spoke up. "I think he said it three times."

"Well, then, why don't you look into all of it, Mr. Police Chief?" Orson asked.

"Because he can't," Ruby said slowly. "You can't launch your own investigation, can you?"

Brett shook his head. "Her fiancé is one of my best officers. This has zero to do with anything in my jurisdiction, aside from Myra's residence," he said. "If I go snooping around in this, it won't look very good. It might even look like I'm meddling in something because I think the Morton County Sheriff is wrong."

"But she is," Orson argued.

"I agree, but that doesn't mean I can do anything about it," Brett said. "Not legally."

"Doesn't mean you can't try," Orson mumbled.

"Actually, it does," Brett raised his voice slightly. "My interference might actually work against Myra if it comes to that."

"I think what Brett is trying to say is that somebody ought to look into all of this, just not him," Jake said.

"I think what I just heard was Brett giving us permission to meddle," Maggie said.

"I never said that." Brett winked at Maggie and then walked back through the kitchen door to the front.

Orson muttered a few more words and then walked off. He headed for the dining room and Jake shrugged his shoulders and followed the older man. Ruby returned to the prep table while Maggie hung around the cooler and tried to block out the thoughts in her head.

"I know this sounds redundant," Ruby said suddenly. "But this is so unfair. This is the last thing Myra needs to deal with right before her wedding. I mean, she was super stressed out by the cake drama. What is this going to do to her?"

Maggie turned around and exhaled. "No, we are not doing this," she said and waved her hand in the air.

"Doing what?" Ruby said.

"Wallowing. And I am quite surprised that it's you who is doing it this time. Typically, that's my line of expertise," Maggie said.

"What do you want me to do, order more flowers for her wedding day that is looking like it isn't going to happen now?"

"This doesn't sound like you."

"What should I sound like, then?" Ruby asked.

"How about, 'let's get out of here as fast as we can so we can go somewhere and figure out what we can do next?' We need to sit and strategize and figure things out!"

Ruby began chopping up vegetables for the second day of her southwestern salads. As Maggie spoke, her chops were louder and harder. "I suppose that is what I would normally say," Ruby said.

"Wonderful. You and I are going to get out of here and put our heads together and see what we can figure out. I'm going to get my things together and then talk to Orson while you finish up."

Maggie went to her office to get her things and then went off to find Orson. She'd been trying to force herself to think about her donut trees to take her mind off other things and had come to a decision.

"Buttercream or cream cheese?" she asked when she found him cleaning one of the tables out front.

"I'm sorry?"

"For the donut tree. Do you think we should fill the donuts with chocolate-cherry buttercream or frost them with a cream cheese icing?"

Without a word, Orson disappeared into the store-room for a minute and returned with a clean white linen tablecloth. He held up a finger and took off again. Moments later, he came back, carrying a small box. He laid out the linen on the table in front of them and began to take items from the box he'd set on the chair. He fanned out the outer edges of the linen, somehow making it look whimsical.

"What are you doing?" Maggie asked him.

"Just wait," Orson said. He set a small Christmas tree in the middle of the white tablecloth. He placed a few artificial flowers around the tree and took off his watch and placed it at the edge of the table. "Give me some of your jewelry," he said.

Maggie handed over her bracelet and two rings, eyeing him carefully. He placed them around the tree and paused, looking around the room. He dashed over to the shelf above the counter and pulled down a snow-globe that Bradley had given his mother as a gift.

"Orson..."

"Shhh," he said as he moved some items around. "What do you think?" he asked finally.

Before Maggie could answer, Ruby came out of the kitchen and rushed over to them. "I have no idea what all this is, but it looks worthy of a spread in Better Homes and Gardens."

"I don't know what this is either," Maggie admitted.

"It's a mock display for your idea. Now, close your eyes and remove the Christmas tree from your mind. What do you see?" Orson asked.

She closed her eyes and seconds later, she was grinning wildly. "Definitely cream cheese."

Ruby glanced back and forth between them and raised a brow. "You see cream cheese when you close your eyes?"

"Absolutely. The buttercream filling will be too heavy. We can frost the donuts and maybe even give them a cherry cordial flavor with the chocolate icing on top."

"What?" Ruby shook her head.

"Good," Orson said. "Now you two get the heck out of here. Jake and I have everything under control."

"What?" Ruby asked again.

"Perfect. I don't know how you do it but thank you, Orson." She gave him a big hug and turned to Ruby. "Are you ready to go?

"Yes, are you ready?" Orson asked, tapping his foot.

Ruby looked at the table again but glanced away quickly. "Why do you want us to leave so badly?"

"Because you aren't going to solve any murders chopping up vegetables or worrying about cream cheese," Orson said. "Now, go! Go figure this out so we can get Myra back home and safe."

Maggie patted Orson gently on the arm. "Message

received," she said. She turned to Ruby. "My house. One hour. Bring your laptop." She removed her apron and tossed it into the dirty clothes hamper inside the storeroom along with the white tablecloth.

"Fine," Ruby said. "But you have to tell me what all that was before we do anything else."

She agreed and headed for her car and drove straight home. Fifteen minutes later, she stood under a steady stream of hot water in her shower and sobbed for her young friend. Maggie was determined to get it all out then and there. When she emerged from the shower, she wiped the fog from the mirror and narrowed her eyes.

"We are not going to act emotionally this time," she told her reflection. "We're going to take a page out of Ruby's book and think logically and get this mess solved quickly."

Maggie dressed quickly in her favorite pair of jeans and a simple button-up shirt. She pulled on her boots in case they needed to go somewhere. She had just pulled her hair back into a low ponytail when she heard a knock on the back door.

"You're early," she sang out and pulled the door open. She expected to see Ruby standing on the other side. Instead, she found the woman who had been at the donut shop earlier that morning, Daisy McNorris. "What are you doing here?" she asked.

"I don't know if you heard, but my friend and business partner was killed this morning," Daisy wailed. She pushed her way past Maggie and went inside. "It's the worst feeling in the world to lose your best friend. Can you get me a cup of coffee, dear?"

Maggie closed the door again and turned back to the kitchen. "I heard about Ms. Reiss and I'm very sorry to have heard about what happened, but what I don't understand is what you are doing here. How do you even know where I live?"

"This is just awful," Daisy continued to wail. "Even a drink of water will do."

Maggie opened her refrigerator and pulled out a bottle of water. "I don't think you heard me, ma'am," she said and handed the water to her. "I don't know you. Why are you here? And as I understood it, you were Ms. Reiss's assistant and her former assistant at that."

"What are you saying?" Daisy said. "Are you accusing me of making up lies?"

"No," Maggie said. Her patience was thinning quickly. "I'm asking you for the last time why you are in my house? I don't know you. I never met Wanda Reiss and I have no idea why you are sitting at my kitchen table crying about this. Don't you have a family member or a friend that you can talk to?"

"I thought I could talk to you," Daisy said. "I never expected for you to be so cold and unfeeling. I also wanted to let you know that you can pay me directly for the services rendered to your friend, Myra. I am taking over her accounts."

Maggie stared at the woman for a full half-minute before she could speak. "You are either very ill or you have lost your mind," she said at last. "I don't owe Ms. Reiss a single penny. I never entered into a contract with her. As far as my friend goes, Wanda canceled the contract they had for the wedding cake and kept her deposit. And as far as I can understand, Myra doesn't owe her another dime."

"Wanda still has an open account with Myra," Daisy said. Her sobs had mysteriously ceased. "You provided the cash for Myra to pay me a deposit for the wedding cake I am going to make for her. That's why I figured you would be good for the rest of the money owed to Wanda."

"I am utterly confused," Maggie said. "Why on earth do you think you are entitled to Ms. Reiss's accounts? And on top of that, why do you think Myra owes her another dime? She never rendered any service to her!"

"I can tell you are getting upset, Maggie," Daisy said, perfectly sanguine. "I will be sending you an invoice soon, so you'll probably want to keep your eyes peeled. Or you can deal with John Michael, my business partner. However, I'll say that it would be in your best interest to deal directly with me."

Maggie watched in disbelief as the woman rose from her chair, swiped the water bottle off of her table, and stalked right back out the door. Ruby had just arrived when the woman backed her car out of the drive and sped off down the road.

"What on earth was that all about?" Ruby asked when she approached the back door.

"Come on in and have a seat," Maggie said. "You're going to need to sit down for this one."

Maggie related what happened when Daisy showed up a few moments before.

"Wait a minute," Ruby said. "How does any of this make sense? Are you sure you heard her correctly?"

"Oh, I heard her alright," Maggie said. "And I just related to you everything she said. Think about it, Ruby. How much doubt do you have about what I told you when you consider the mere fact that she showed up at my house in the first place?"

Ruby nodded her head. "Yeah, good point," she

said. She took a seat in the same chair Daisy had occupied and opened her laptop on the table. "I'm sorry I doubted you, Maggie. I'm way more emotional about all of this than usual. I think I'm too close to the situation."

"You're just really close to Myra, and I understand that," Maggie said. "I know you don't have any kids of your own, but I think Myra comes close to that for you. I've been emotional when it comes to Bradley before. You've been up close and personal to that."

"I suppose you're right," Ruby replied.

"I am." Maggie smiled. "Now, let's get busy and figure some things out."

Maggie disappeared into her bedroom and returned with her own computer. She sat across from Ruby and opened the lid.

"I can't find a business listing of any kind for Wanda Reiss's cake business," Ruby announced when Maggie sat down. "I mean, there's nothing."

"Did you check social media? I assume that's how Myra found her."

"Nothing on Facebook, Instagram, nothing," Ruby said. She opened her laptop bag and pulled out her cell phone. "I'm going to text Brooks and ask him if he has any idea how she found this woman."

"Do you think that's a good idea? I don't want to upset him any more than he already is," Maggie said.

"I have a feeling nothing is going to be more upsetting to him than his future wife being accused of murder."

CHAPTER SEVEN

Maggie continued to search through every directory she could think to look into for any shred of evidence of Wanda Reiss's cake business. She turned to newspapers around Joplin, and then southern Missouri at large but found nothing.

When Brooks did not return her text, Ruby suggested reaching out to Brett. "It's possible Myra has been arrested and Brooks is visiting her in the Morton County jail," she said. "I don't want to think that way, but I also don't want to waste a lot of time wondering."

"I agree." Maggie stood and picked up her phone from the counter next to the sink. She opened her texting app and sent Brett a short message. He replied within seconds.

"Okay if I stop by?" he asked. "I'm two blocks away."

"Of course," she answered and set the phone down on the table. "We're about to have a visitor. Brett is down the block."

"Good timing," Ruby said.

Maggie waited until she saw Brett's car pull into her driveway and opened the door for him.

"Please tell me you have something cold to drink," he said as he came in. "I swear these temperature changes are going to drive me crazy. I barely know how to dress."

Maggie laughed at him as he removed his jacket. "We can have a lesson in layering clothing later, if you want."

"I'll get the drinks," Ruby called from the kitchen. Maggie heard the sound of the water running into the coffee carafe.

"Brooks is in Morton County," Brett said right away. "I haven't heard anything about Myra yet, though."

"Something weird is going on," Maggie said. "Daisy McNorris stopped by here about an hour ago."

"That's one of the cake ladies, right?" Brett asked.

"She has called herself both Wanda Reiss's business partner and her assistant," Maggie said. "And she showed up here and just pushed her way inside. She started bawling about losing her best friend and then turned the waterworks off and demanded payment from me on Wanda's behalf! Wanda never did a thing for Myra, and she kept her deposit."

"I thought the whole reason Myra was in contact with this Daisy woman was because of Wanda flaking out on the wedding cake in the first place," Brett said with a blank stare on his face.

"It is," Maggie said. "Which is why none of what she said made any sense. It was utter nonsense and she spewed it out like she was testifying in front of a judge."

"What else did she say, aside from demanding money from you?" he asked.

"Basically, she said she was going to send me an invoice for payment and that I better play ball with her or face her business partner, John Michael," Maggie said.

"Wait. I thought you said she was partnered with Reiss," Brett said.

"Now you're starting to get it," Maggie said. "The woman made zero sense."

"I would say so," Brett said. "What did you need with Brooks?"

"We were wondering how Myra came across

Wanda in the first place," Ruby said from the kitchen. "Our drinks are ready, by the way. I made toffee-nut iced coffee and the ice cubes are made from coffee so our drinks won't get watered down."

"Thanks, Ruby," he called. "I'm surprised you two didn't think to find her business online yet," Brett said, glancing at the open computers.

"We looked, but there wasn't a thing about her business," Ruby said. "I don't know how Myra found out about these people."

"Is it possible that they used a business name you just didn't realize was theirs?" Brett asked as they made their way into the kitchen.

"I suppose anything is possible, but there's a website that lists businesses and their owners, along with contact information and annual revenue," Ruby said. "I checked every baker within a hundred miles of here and in Joplin. I found nothing associated with Wanda or Daisy or anybody named John Michael."

Maggie went to the fridge for creamer. She added a splash to each of the glasses and decided at the last minute to add whipped cream to the top of the iced coffees. "Something just isn't right here," she said at last. "I wish I could put my finger on it."

"I think we've covered that," Brett said. "Isn't that what we've been talking about?"

Maggie shook her head. "No, it's something more. More than not being able to find the business name or trying to understand what Daisy was going on and on about."

"What do you mean?" Ruby asked. "Can you be more specific?"

Maggie shook her head. She sat down in her chair and circled her mug with her hands. "I can't be more specific," she said. "It's just a feeling I have. A terrible, awful, foreboding feeling."

"So, you have a bad feeling, but you don't know why or what the feeling is about?" Brett asked as he stirred the whipped cream into his glass.

"They're mostly always right," Ruby said, attempting to defend her friend.

"I get it." Brett nodded. "But you have to forgive me for being skeptical. As I've said several times before, feelings aren't something the police can go on all the time. We need evidence to back up those feelings."

"Are you struggling with not having control over this situation, Brett?" Ruby asked.

He continued to stir in the whipped cream that had long since melted, and eventually looked up. "I guess I am. It's hard because it involves Brooks so neither one of us can participate or even ask any questions.

And then, of course, because of Myra and how close she is to both of you. It's not easy to do nothing, if that makes sense."

Maggie smiled at him softly. "It makes perfect sense and it's why I can't get this awful feeling to go away. I'm worried that these cake people have some sort of money scam going on and Myra might just get taken by them and it's not fair."

Ruby cleared her throat and opened her mouth to speak but quickly shut it.

"Are you trying to hold back from saying 'I told you so'?" Maggie asked.

"I wouldn't dare."

CHAPTER EIGHT

"Did you find any personal social media profiles for this woman?" Gretchen LeClair asked Maggie the following morning. With Myra still gone, Maggie decided to make the run to the Dogwood House, the local bed and breakfast, and her Aunt Marjorie's grand former home. Gretchen was the proud owner and a good friend who was appreciative of the daily deliveries made by the donut shop for both breakfast and lunch each day.

"Nothing," Maggie admitted. Late into the night, she had looked along with Ruby for any evidence that Wanda Reiss had ever had a wedding cake business. "I don't know if she is just an older woman who didn't want a social media footprint, or what."

"Ouch," Gretchen said. She helped herself to a

vanilla scone and a cup of coffee. "I have profiles on everything, both personal and business-related."

"You know what I mean," Maggie said, blushing slightly. She had not meant to insult anyone. "Even my generation didn't grow up with social media as a part of our lives. Not until we were older. Some people never get involved with it and that's perfectly fine. It's just unfortunate because I need this woman to have a footprint, and she doesn't."

Gretchen sipped more coffee and shook her head. "But can you really imagine a service-based company like a bakery for wedding cakes not having a social presence? Most of the people I run into in the culinary world are all over the social media landscape. I just don't know how you'd even avoid it."

"I don't know, but I think I need to go see Myra today," Maggie said. "I'm not sure they'll even let me see her, but I have to at least try."

"I can't imagine how devastated she is," Gretchen said. "Brooks, too. Have they charged her with anything?"

"I honestly don't know," Maggie said. "Brett was over until late last night and he hadn't heard, either. He said they don't have much time left to hold her before they have to let her go or charge her with something."

"None of this seems fair," Gretchen said. "I truly do hope this is all cleared up soon and we are able to witness those two getting married. I adore young Myra, and Brooks is such a good young man."

"Not to mention the lovely dress you get to wear." Maggie smiled. "Mrs. Pennyworth made mention of it when she was at my house measuring a very grumpy older man earlier this week."

"That's Orson," Gretchen said. "I wish he would just be okay with moving in here. But as we all know, he's not much for public displays of… well, anything, but I've never met someone who moves so slowly in all my years. I'm not talking marriage or anything, and we wouldn't even share a room, but he's just absolutely refusing my offer. I hate to think that he's sitting in that house of his, warmer than who knows what, and doing nothing but waiting for Myra to move out. It's just a shame."

"So, he officially told you no?"

"Sure did. He said that he'd never burden me like that, and I should be using my extra rooms for guests."

"Do you think…" Maggie paused. "Do you think he wants to move away from Dogwood Mountain for good?"

Gretchen whipped her head around to face

Maggie. "Did he say something about moving to you?"

Right away, she worried she'd said too much. The last thing she wanted to do was get in the middle of their relationship but swore to herself she'd do all she could to keep Orson in town. "Nothing specific, I guess, but I'm worried it might be an option for him and I really don't want him to leave. If you hear anything, please encourage him to stay."

"You bet I will. There is no way that man is leaving. I always give him space but not with this." Gretchen stomped her foot. "I've got this handled. Don't you worry."

After being assured three more times that Gretchen would make sure Orson stuck around, Maggie pulled out of the driveway at the Dogwood House and headed back toward the donut shop. She thought over Gretchen's words as she drove. What she needed to do the most, she decided, was pay a visit to the Morton County Jail. If she was lucky, she would get to see Myra and get to the bottom of some of the odd circumstances surrounding the dead woman.

Ruby stood guard at the baker's table when Maggie walked back through the back door. "How was Miss Gretchen?" Ruby asked.

Orson stood facing the sink. His shoulders froze in place at the mention of Gretchen's name. "She's worried about Myra, of course," Maggie said.

"Have you heard anything from Brooks this morning?" Orson asked.

"Not a word," Maggie admitted. "But I'm going to reach out to Brett if I don't hear something by the middle of the morning rush. I think one of us needs to pay Myra a visit over in Morton County as soon as we can."

"You know, Maggie," Ruby said and turned toward her. She brushed the flour off of the front of her apron. "I think one of us should run to the restaurant supply store in Joplin later today."

"What do you want to go to the restaurant supply store for?" Maggie asked.

"Personally? I want to go and pick up baking supplies for a tiered wedding cake," Ruby said. "I have the ingredients at home for the chocolate raspberry cake Myra wanted and I truly do not put a whole lot of faith into this Daisy woman."

Maggie smiled despite her doubts about the wedding taking place. She wanted to bury her head in her arms and weep out of relief for Ruby's stubborn belief that it was still going to happen. "I love this plan," she said, trying to hide the emotion in her voice.

"The other reason is that if there is a wedding cake baker around the Joplin area, the chances are Theresa at the restaurant supply store is going to know of him or her," Ruby said. "She will have at least heard of them."

Orson turned around from the sink and pointed his finger directly at Ruby. "Now that is some good thinking," he said. "And at noon, the two of you can just get on your way. Go together and stop at the jail on your way. I have Jake here with me to handle things until close." He turned back around and resumed washing the large metal baking sheet he had been working on.

"I guess we have our orders." Maggie chuckled. "Are you sure you want to close up today, Orson?" He replied with a stern stare over his shoulder.

"I guess we have our answer," Ruby said. She turned back to her own work on the scones in front of her.

"I think I'll see to the donut machines," Maggie announced. "I think we're going to need a few extra chocolate cake donuts this morning."

"Good plan," Orson muttered without looking around.

Soon after, Maggie opened the front doors and stared out at the parking lot, still dark in the early morning hours. She smiled at the sight of The Diner, Flo Johnson's food truck parked on the other side of the lot beneath the tall donut shop sign. Her own food truck was tucked neatly away in the alley behind the building. Myra had done so much to promote both trucks. Her work with Flo practically saved the business from the start.

Maggie inhaled deeply and turned back to the counter. Already, headlights glowed in the parking lot as customers began to arrive. Maggie welcomed the distraction. Her thoughts of Myra threatened to leave her in tears.

By eight, the dining room was filled to capacity. A line of customers stretched all the way to the front doors. Maggie worked as fast as she could alongside Orson, who had come up front and practically taken over the morning rush. When the line died down at last Maggie spotted Brett, dressed in full uniform, walking down the sidewalk and into the donut shop. He nodded at Orson and locked eyes with Maggie. There was not even a hint of a smile in his eyes.

"You look like the bearer of very bad news," Maggie said when he was close enough to the counter.

"I wish I had better news," he said.

Maggie turned and retrieved two cinnamon rolls from the display case. "Here or to go?"

"To go," Brett said. "I have a lot to do today. I made Brooks stay home again. He is dealing with some pressure from his family over this whole thing."

"His family?"

Brett nodded. "Apparently his aunt is having a conniption fit over Myra being in trouble again," he said. "She caught wind of Myra's earlier troubles when she first came to town and has now decided that the wedding should not proceed. Not now, not ever."

"I don't see how anyone can blame her for what happened to her in the past," Maggie said. "And this time is no different. We both know Myra didn't kill Wanda so unless you're telling me otherwise, that woman has no right to say anything."

"I agree, but you and I are not exactly unbiased when it comes to those two," Brett said. "Which is precisely why I can't help in this investigation in any way."

Maggie nodded. This was old news to her. "I'm well aware of that," she said. "And so is Ruby."

"Okay, good." Brett glanced up at Orson who had prepared a cinnamon latte for him. "Thank you."

"Uh-huh," Orson muttered when he set the drink

down in front of him.

"To another point," Brett said. "Have you come up with anything on your end?"

"Well, I planned on leaving here after lunch to see if they let me visit Myra and then I'll be driving with Ruby up to the restaurant supply store in Joplin for wedding cake supplies," Maggie said. "And to ask around a bit about the people who were going to make Myra's cake."

Brett nodded. "I don't think you'll have any luck seeing Myra, but the rest sounds like a very good idea," he said. "And a very full afternoon."

"The restaurant supply store closes at five. She will be back no later than six and will be happy to accompany you to dinner tonight," Orson said over her head.

Maggie turned around and faced him. "Orson!"

"That's a fine idea." Brett leaned forward on the counter and rested his hand close to hers. "Do you want to have dinner with me tonight?"

"Of course, I do. But I actually plan to be back much sooner than that. I'll give you a call or shoot you a text when we leave Joplin."

"I can't wait. See you soon Detective Sharpe." The way Brett finger quoted the word detective had Orson in stitches.

CHAPTER NINE

As promised, Orson rushed Ruby and Maggie out the
door shortly after lunchtime. Jake worked feverishly
to follow the older man's directions.

"Sometimes I think we are going to wind up obso-
lete in our own business," Maggie said to Ruby as
they pulled out of the alley. They were in Ruby's
pickup truck. Her own car was still in the shop and
neither one wanted to make the long drive to Joplin in
Beastly Beulah.

"We might want to call ahead and make sure we
can get in to see her," Ruby said about twelve miles
outside of Dogwood Mountain. "I know. I should
have thought about that before."

"I didn't think about it, either," Maggie said. She
googled the phone number. She called the jail and

waited while the recording played. A second later, the line went dead.

"What happened?"

"The recording said to come to the administration building and check-in for visitors between eight in the morning and five in the afternoon. After that, the line went dead," Maggie said. "I'm going to call back and find out if Myra can even have visitors."

"If I remember correctly, they won't tell you anything specific about an inmate," Ruby said. "We might as well just wait until we get there."

"I guess it isn't a waste of time since we're headed in that direction anyway," Maggie said.

An hour later, Maggie waited while Ruby pulled her identification out of her small bag. Maggie stood ready with her own. They agreed to leave their cell phones locked up in the truck.

They approached the desk inside the administration section of the jail and gave the secretary Myra's name.

"Myra Sawyer isn't here," the woman said.

"Is that what people say when someone can't have visitors?" Ruby asked.

"No, when someone can't have visitors, we say they can't have visitors. What I'm saying now is that Myra Sawyer is no longer here."

"Where is she?" Maggie asked.

"How would I know? I'm not the keeper of people when they are here and I'm certainly not their keeper when they leave. Myra Sawyer, whoever she is to you, is not here." The woman barely looked up from her desk.

They stepped away from where they stood and looked at each other blankly. "If she's not here, does that mean she was charged and had to go talk to someone?"

"Or maybe they found out the truth and let her go," Maggie said with hope bubbling up inside of her.

Before either of them could figure out what to do next, a woman came over to them. "Is the girl you're looking for young?"

Maggie turned to face the newcomer. "Yes, why?"

"Longish, dark hair? Wearing a blue shirt?" the woman asked.

"Umm, yeah, maybe. Why are you asking?" Ruby demanded.

"Because I've been here waiting for a visit, and I noticed a younger woman who had just gotten out. It didn't seem like she was getting out of a long-term stay or anything and you two don't look like you were expecting an inmate who wasn't going to be here. You also look upset and like you want to find her."

"Yes, that's true. What else can you tell us about her?" Maggie asked. "Maybe we can figure out if it's the same person."

"You're in luck because the car that took her away just happens to belong to my cousin, Felix."

"What do you mean took her away?" Ruby panicked. "Are you saying someone…"

"No, no," the woman rolled her eyes. "I'm saying that Felix works for a car service. He dropped me off here for my visit and ended up taking your girl wherever it is that she was going."

Maggie looked at Ruby with wide eyes. "So, can you call Felix or something and find out if it was the same person we are looking for?"

The woman looked at the ceiling and then her feet. She sighed a few times and finally spoke. "I could."

"Okay, great!" Maggie exclaimed. She turned to Ruby. "This is such good news. What if it's her?"

Ruby nodded but then turned her attention the other woman. "Do you need to borrow one of our phones or something?"

"I have a phone," the woman said, still not moving to make the call.

Ruby muttered something under her breath then dug her hand into her bag. "You want money?" The woman shrugged but then held out her hand. Ruby handed over a twenty and put her hands on her hips. "Go ahead."

The woman looked at Maggie next, her hand still out.

"Are you kidding?" Maggie asked, reaching into her own bag. She slapped the money in the woman's hand.

"Thanks so much for offering cash. That was so kind of you both." The woman pulled out her phone and dialed. She stepped away when she began to talk.

Not long after, the woman returned. "Her name Myra?"

Maggie nodded frantically. "Yes! Where did she go? The donut shop? Home?"

The woman gave her a look of pure disgust. "No, Felix didn't bring her for donuts. She went to the Morton County Motel. That's all I know so don't ask me any more questions." She stalked off to the desk to ask when she'd finally get to have her visit.

"Let's get to the truck so we can find this motel. We've got to get to Myra." Ruby led the way.

"Why would she go there and not home? Why wouldn't she have called one of us? Do you think Brooks knows she's out?" Maggie rattled off her questions as they walked.

"I don't know any more than you do," Ruby said as she opened her door. Right away, she pulled out her phone and searched the GPS for the Morton County Motel. "I've got it. Buckle up and let's go."

Ten minutes later, they rushed into the lobby of a small motel. The man behind the front counter looked up at them with surprise. "Is everything okay, ladies?" he asked.

Maggie glanced at his name tag. "Bobby, we're looking for a friend of ours. We think she just checked in and we have her phone. We wanted to make sure she got it." She held up her own phone, hoping her plan worked.

"You're more than welcome to leave it here with me and I'll contact her in her room to let her know."

"Can't you just tell us what room she's in?" Maggie asked, already knowing the answer.

Bobby forced a smile. "Unfortunately, that's against our policy. Like I said, if your friend is, in fact, a guest here, I'll be happy to call to her room to let her know I have her phone."

"Okay. Is it okay if we wait here?" Ruby asked.

"I suppose it will be okay if you go wait in your car or something. It's of the utmost importance that we keep our guests safe. It's best if you two fine ladies give me the name of your friend, then step outside. If for some reason, she is here but doesn't want to see you, then you will be free to go on your way."

"Jeez. This place has more rules than the jail," Maggie mumbled.

Bobby eyed her with pure fear coming over his face at her mention of the word jail.

"Why don't you head outside, and I'll give Bobby what he needs." Ruby directed Maggie out the door.

Maggie did as she was asked but stared hard through the lobby window. A minute later, she saw Ruby heading off further into the lobby and saw Bobby dialing the phone. She noticed Ruby look over her shoulder and was about to race into the lobby to see what was going on. If he let Ruby back to find Myra, she was going to be so mad.

Her phone buzzed in her hand. She read the text from Ruby. "I said I had to use the restroom, but I was able to get a look at the number Bobby dialed. It was either a 2 or a 4 which means Myra is probably in one of those rooms. I'm trying to check their website to see how many rooms this place has total, but the Wi-Fi is junk in here. I'll be out soon."

Maggie giggled with excitement at Ruby's find. She searched around until she found the website for the motel, learning that there were fourteen rooms in the place. She wasn't sure why Ruby wanted to know, but she'd find out soon enough.

"Okay, so let me see if I can get some Wi-Fi out here," Ruby said when she came outside.

"There are fourteen rooms, but what did Bobby say? Is Myra even staying here?"

"Forget him. I told him we ended up getting in touch with her. You said there are fourteen rooms and I know for a fact I saw him hit either the 2 or the 4 button. I didn't get a perfect look, but from my time working at a hotel restaurant, I know how to dial a room. If Myra is here, then she's in a room that ends in one of those numbers."

"So, now what? Are you suggesting that we knock on all the doors or something?"

"Maybe, but first let me try something." Ruby dialed a number and headed for her truck.

Maggie chased after her, entirely confused as to what was going on. "Ruby."

"Okay, so Myra isn't in room 12 or 14," she said a few minutes later. "That means she has to be in 2 or 4."

"How do you know?" Maggie asked.

"Well, I'm out eighty-six dollars, but I just called to book a room here at the motel. I asked if room 12 or 14 were vacant because they're my favorite. Bobby told me they were both vacant and I could take my pick of the two."

"Are you crazy?" Maggie couldn't help but laugh. "You could have told him you'd call back after deciding which room you wanted."

Ruby chuckled. "I wasn't thinking straight, I guess. But we know now that if Myra is here, she's likely in room 2 or 4. That's more than we knew before."

Maggie heard a noise that sounded like a soft yelp. She turned her head in the direction of the noise and swore she saw Myra standing in the doorway. "Myra!" she shouted and began running.

Ruby followed close behind and when she caught up to Maggie, she was banging on the door to room number 4.

"Myra! Myra! I know it's you in there. I saw your face," Maggie said as loudly as she could, not wanting to disrupt the other guests or get in trouble.

Ruby gently nudged her out of the way. "Are you sure it was her?" she whispered.

"Ninety-nine percent," Maggie answered.

Ruby gently knocked on the door. "Myra, please. Let us in. We just want to talk to you and make sure you're okay."

They heard rustling behind the door, but no one opened it.

"Myra, please, we don't have a lot of time," Maggie begged. "I need to ask you about Wanda Reiss. How did you come to find out about her baking services? We have been looking into things and cannot find a company listed anywhere."

"I think she's crying," Ruby said pressing her ear against the door. "Myra, please, let us help you."

"That's because she makes wedding cakes in her own kitchen," Myra's voice was muffled. "I got her name and number from the lady I found on social media. She had a wedding dress for sale, and I talked to her on the phone, though I never tried on the dress. Turns out it wasn't the style I wanted."

"Oh, Myra! It's you," Maggie cried. "Are you okay? Can you let us in?"

"No. I don't want to see anyone right now. Not you guys, not Brooks. I don't think there's even going to be a wedding. There's no way Brooks will still want to marry me after all this."

"What are you talking about? Of course, he wants to marry you. Brooks loves you," Maggie assured her.

"Not according to his aunt. She called me and left me a very clear voice message. Brooks and I aren't getting married. Now, please, leave me alone. I'll find you all when I'm ready. Unless the police come up with something more against me. Then who knows where I'll be."

"Myra…" Maggie began, trying to turn the doorknob.

Ruby shook her head. "We will leave you alone, but can you help us with just one thing first?"

"What?" Myra asked through her tears.

"Do you still have the number for the wedding dress lady? Or can you remember her name?" Ruby asked.

"Theresa," Myra mumbled through the door. "She lives in Hunter Springs and works for the restaurant supply store in Joplin. The dress she had needed a lot of alterations, and I just didn't have time. I think she felt bad, so she gave me Wanda's number for the cake. But none of it matters now. I'm not in jail, but there won't be a wedding." The sobs were louder now.

"Thank you for the help, Myra," Ruby said. "Do you want us to let Brooks know you're okay?"

"Don't bother. He won't care."

CHAPTER TEN

Ruby drove on toward Joplin without saying a word. By the time they pulled into the parking lot of the store, Maggie unbuckled her seatbelt and turned sideways to face her.

"You haven't said a single word since we left the motel," Maggie said. "Please tell me you aren't angry with me because I encouraged Myra to let us in or that I pushed her too hard when she just wanted to be left alone."

Ruby shook her head. "I'm not angry," she said. "At least, not with you. I'm just so mad about what is happening to Myra. I'm so thankful she was let out, but I don't know if that means she's free from all charges in the future or not. I hate that she thinks

Brooks doesn't want to marry her and I'm livid that someone had the gall to tell her as much."

"What do you mean free of future charges?" Maggie asked.

"They might have just been forced to let her out because they had nothing against her. But that doesn't mean they have something on someone else, either. I don't think I'll feel better until they figure out who did this."

"Myra might be going through something hard right now, but the truth will come out. She is a strong woman who doesn't have to do this on her own," Maggie reminded her. "She just needs a little time alone to remember that. And just because she doesn't want us in the motel room with her, doesn't mean we aren't going to support her from afar."

Ruby patted the steering wheel with her palms and smiled. "You're right. I need to remember that and have some faith," she said. "I say only one of us talks to Theresa. She might feel like we're ganging up on her if we both try. Do you want to do it? Maybe not knowing her will help us out somehow."

"Okay," Maggie agreed.

They walked into the store and went their separate ways. Maggie grabbed a basket from the display near the entrance. She walked around the bakery section for several moments. She placed three round tins in her basket and moved to the sheet pans. She would gladly leave the flavors and icing colors to Ruby.

"Can I help you?" a woman called from behind her. She was dressed in a pair of khakis and a polo with the store's logo embroidered on the breast pocket. Maggie searched for a name tag.

"I am helping a friend with a wedding cake," she said. "I own a donut shop in Dogwood Mountain."

"Oh, are you a full-service bakery, too?"

Maggie shook her head. "Not exactly," she said. "I have the commercial kitchen to make it in, and my business partner is an experienced chef, but this is a favor."

"Oh, I see," the woman said. "Well, if I can help you find something, let me know."

"Actually, my friend said someone who works here gave her the name of a lady who bakes wedding cakes out of her kitchen," Maggie said.

"You mean the same woman who was found dead in her car?"

"I do," Maggie said, feeling her stomach drop.

"Are you a cop?" the woman asked.

"Not at all," Maggie said. "I really have a donut shop and the bride is one of my employees. Actually, she is more than that. She is family and she is dealing with something difficult right now because of her connection with this woman."

"So, you're here to see if you can find some super-secret information from the lady that gave her the contact info in the first place?"

"I'm here because I know this girl and she didn't kill anyone," Maggie said. She felt the beads of sweat gather on her forehead. "And because another woman who claims to be a business partner or a personal assistant barged into my house and threatened me if I didn't pay her for the cake Ms. Reiss never made."

"That's weird," the woman said.

"Oh, it gets even weirder," Maggie said. She felt her heart racing in her chest and just let everything pour out. "This same woman had also made arrangements with the bride, to bail her out after Wanda flaked out on her. I gave her several hundred dollars down as a deposit, and she took that, too!"

"Alright, I get it," the woman said. She walked toward a small register in the middle of the store and pulled a piece of paper from under the counter. She scrawled something on the page and handed it to Maggie. "I have no idea what is going on, but that's the number some lady gave me and said she had a home-based bakery. She came in here a few months ago and said she had just moved to the Joplin area and hoped to start up her wedding cake business here."

"And you have been giving out her number to brides-to-be as a favor?"

"Yeah, and she has come in here and spent a lot of money on supplies, which is good because we work on commission, plus a minimal salary," she said. "I didn't really remember much about her, but the police showed me a picture of the victim and that was the same woman."

"Are you Theresa? And did you recently have a wedding dress for sale on Facebook?"

"That's my name," she said. "Why do you want to know my name?"

"Oh, just because that's one of the few things Myra recalled about where she heard about this woman," Maggie explained. "Is there anything else at all that you can remember about her? Did she have someone else with her?"

Theresa leaned her elbows on the counter. "The only thing I remember is that she said something about having had a bakery somewhere before. I don't know when or where that might have been, but she wanted to start her own business from home because she didn't want to work with employees or staff anymore," she said.

"And you have no idea where she might have been from? Not even a state?"

Theresa seemed to think hard. "Hang on," she said and began pulling more scraps of paper from beneath the counter. "I thought I might have had a note here. The same lady called me back and asked me to use a new number instead. I just end up giving people both numbers most of the time. I can't remember which one is the right one anyhow."

Ruby walked past them just as Maggie said goodbye to Theresa. "Any luck?" she asked when they were out of earshot.

"Maybe. Theresa confirmed pretty much what Myra said."

"Okay, so what else did she say?"

"She said that some woman came in here a few months ago and left her name and number so she could give it out to customers who might be looking for a wedding cake baker," Maggie said.

"So, you have the name and number, but that would be Wanda's and not all that much help."

"Actually, I have two numbers. The deal was that Theresa would tell people about this woman's home bakery business, and the woman would buy all of her supplies from this store while Theresa was on the clock because of commission or something," Maggie said. "But then she said the same woman called her back with a new number to use, but that she couldn't really remember which was which, so she just gave out both."

Ruby studied the pans behind her. "These are actually what I need and not those," she said pointing to the pans in Maggie's basket.

"You don't seem too excited," Maggie said. "We got the numbers for two people and my guess is that one of them belongs to Daisy McNorris."

"That's good and I am glad that we came here," Ruby said. "But those numbers really don't make any sense."

"What do you mean? Just because we didn't get their names to go with them? I'm sure Brett or Brooks can look up who they belong to," Maggie said.

"No. It isn't that," Ruby said. "Think about it. Why would a wedding cake baker drum up business at a restaurant supply store where other bakers shop? This isn't a store that particularly caters to the public."

Maggie sighed and put the pans back she'd chosen. She knew what Ruby was getting at but refused to believe that getting those phone numbers meant nothing.

CHAPTER ELEVEN

Ruby dropped Maggie back at the donut shop shortly after four. She copied the numbers Theresa had given her and handed them to Ruby with the plan to put their heads together later and see if they came up with anything.

Once she was inside the house, Maggie raced through a quick shower and pulled on a simple skirt and tunic. "It's open," she said when a knock came on the door.

Brett stepped inside, dressed in a pair of black slacks and a dark blue button-up shirt, open at the neck.

"You look nice," he said when Maggie stepped into his view.

"So do you," she said. She stood with her hand on

the kitchen table for a long, awkward moment in silence. Brett appeared to be unsure what to say as well. No matter how many dates they had, there was something unsettled between them. Maggie consistently felt like a school girl around Brett, and she suspected he felt something similar.

"Did you find anything out when you went to see Myra?" he asked at last.

Maggie slowly sat down and looked up at Brett. She explained everything to him and waited patiently for him to compose himself. "She's in hiding?"

"I don't know if I'd call it that, but she's out of the direct line of the police for now, it seems. I think she needs some time alone because she truly believes that marrying Brooks will do nothing but cause him harm and bother his family. Myra is very considerate of other people's feelings, and I don't think she could live with herself if she thought Brooks would have to essentially choose between her and his family."

"Brooks wouldn't want her to feel that way. He needs to know," Brett said, sitting down next to Maggie.

"I agree completely. Brooks loves Myra and deep down, I think she knows that, but she's just not ready. She's had nothing but trouble since they started planning this wedding and I believe she needs some time to process on her own. She's in a safe place, Ruby and I know where she is, and it's not our place to get involved."

Brett shook his head. "No. We need to at least tell Brooks that she's safe. It's the right thing to do."

Maggie thought about it for a moment, knowing Brett was right. "Okay," she agreed. "You can tell him she's okay and Ruby and I will talk to her to see if we can convince her to come home."

"Fair. Now, let's talk about those phone numbers," Brett said. "This Theresa woman gave them to you, and she claims to have gotten them from Wanda?"

"Right. Wanda agreed to buy the supplies from Theresa if Theresa agreed to give her number out to customers," Maggie explained again.

"Okay, and both of these numbers belong to Wanda?" Brett asked. "I'd understand if she used one phone for her business and one personal but based on the fact that she ran her business out of her kitchen, it would seem strange for her to have two phones."

"So, what are you thinking? Ruby said she thought it was weird in general because it's not like the restaurant supply store is a place regular people go."

"Good point. There likely aren't very many brides

coming in to buy supplies to make their own wedding cakes, but what I'm thinking is more along the lines of the two phone numbers. It doesn't make a whole lot of sense. Is Theresa sure it was Wanda who gave them to her?"

"You mean Daisy!" Maggie exclaimed. "Theresa said Wanda came in the first time, but said for the second phone number, that the person called in to give it to her. What if it was Daisy?"

"Have you tried to call either number?"

"No, and I don't know if Ruby tried, either," Maggie said. "I got right into the shower when I got home and haven't had the chance."

"Do you have your laptop handy?" Brett asked. "If you don't mind, I can look it up for you."

"Of course," Maggie said. She ducked into her bedroom and returned with the laptop. She set it on the coffee table and signed in. "Here you go."

"Hang on," Brett said. "I have a few resources I can access and look up who these numbers belong to."

While Brett worked on the computer, Maggie's phone rang. "I have to take this," she announced. "It's Ruby. I don't think she would call right now unless it was important." Brett nodded and waved at her from in front of the computer.

"Hi, Ruby," Maggie said. She stepped into the living room to take the call.

"I'm so sorry," Ruby said. "I know you're in the middle of the date with Brett."

"Well, sorta," Maggie said, leaving out the fact that they were just discussing the investigation and not having any romantic moments. "What's up?"

Ruby sighed. "I just got a call from Devin Reynolds, the attorney I'd retained for Myra. He called to inform me that the police are looking for Myra so they can officially charge her with the murder of Wanda Reiss."

"Oh, goodness," Maggie said. Tears immediately streamed down her face. "How can they charge her with murder?"

"I have no idea," Ruby cried. "All I know is that I told Devin where she was just because I didn't want her to end up with a warrant or something. I feel terrible. I can't believe I did that."

"You didn't do anything wrong. It was the right choice," Maggie assured her. "Do you know what evidence they can possibly have on her?"

"They don't, at least according to Devin," Ruby said. "It's all circumstantial and he thinks the case is flimsy at best. But that doesn't help her out right now."

"Hey, Maggie," Brett called from the other room. "Can you come in here?"

"Hold on, Ruby," Maggie said. "Brett is on my computer looking up to the numbers Theresa gave me."

"Oh, okay, good," Ruby said, already sounding calmer.

Maggie returned to the kitchen. She quickly explained what she knew about Myra and sat next to Brett. "Did you find something?" she asked, almost betting that the second number belonged to Daisy.

"I did. This first number does belong to a Wanda Reiss," Brett said.

"Hold on," Maggie said. She set the phone on the table and turned it on speaker. "Can you hear well enough, Ruby?"

"I can," she said.

"Go on," Maggie said to Brett.

"Okay," he continued. "The other number belongs to a man by the name of John Michael McNorris."

"John Michael McNorris? Is he a relative of Daisy's?" Ruby asked.

"Give me a second," Brett said.

"Well, this changes things," Maggie said into the phone. "If the second number Theresa was given came from John Michael McNorris, that definitely ties him to Wanda Reiss and casts a huge shadow of doubt over the idea that Myra was somehow involved with Wanda's death."

"John Michael and Daisy McNorris are husband and wife," Brett announced. "And Wanda's full name was Wanda McNorris Reiss."

"I think I need to sit down," Maggie said. Her head spun from the information.

"How was Wanda related to John Michael?" Ruby asked.

"I'm still looking," Brett replied, running his hands over his face.

"I think we need to place a phone call to the Morton County Sheriff's Department," Maggie said, interrupting everything.

"It pains me to say this, but I think I have to get going." Brett sighed. "I hate to end our date here, but I think the direction is heading away from what we intended on meeting here for."

"But what should we do?" Maggie asked.

"Unfortunately, I can't tell you what to do," Brett admitted.

"So," Ruby said through the phone. "Are you suggesting that we don't go to the police or are you saying you have to leave because you can't be a part of this?"

"Yes," Brett said as he stood.

"You're saying yes to both?" Maggie shook her head.

"I think we should go find these people first," Ruby said,

"Why wouldn't we just call the sheriff?" Maggie asked.

"Because they're going to act completely differently in front of the police," Brett said as he inched closer to the door. "But here's the thing. The address associated with the second phone number is right here within the city limits. That means I get to go with you. But I don't think they're going to recognize the Chief of Police in regular clothes."

"Do you want me to meet you and go with the two of you?" Ruby asked.

"Why don't you meet us at the donut shop as soon as you can get there," Brett said. "You and Maggie can go with the guise of paying for the rest of the wedding cake. I'll sit in the car until I'm needed."

CHAPTER TWELVE

Ruby was waiting for them when Brett and Maggie arrived at the donut shop. Maggie announced that she was going to run into the office and pull more cash out of the safe to back up the story they planned to tell Daisy and John Michael when they arrived at their house.

They agreed to drive in two vehicles to the address Brett found. They also agreed to take Brett's car and Ruby's truck and leave Beastly Beulah parked behind Maggie's house.

"Why don't you ride with Brett?" Ruby said. "Then it will look like you and I met here to drop off the deposit and you just happened to have someone with you."

"Good idea," Brett said. He opened the passenger door for Maggie.

"Thank you," Maggie said.

Brett drove out of the alley and headed for downtown. The address was on the northern outskirts of Dogwood Mountain. Ruby followed close behind.

"This isn't the date I had in mind for us," he said as he drove.

Maggie smiled. "No, but if this turns out well maybe we can find some extra time for each other once Myra and Brooks are back from their honeymoon."

"That sounds like a good plan," Brett said. "But if it's alright with you, I'd like to go on a few dates between now and then."

"Obviously." Maggie laughed. "I just meant maybe Myra can cover for me at the donut shop and we can take a weekend away or something."

"I like the sound of that," Brett said. He followed the main road until the street lights disappeared.

"Is this still in the city limits?" Maggie asked when they turned down a dark street.

"Barely, but yes, it is," he said. "Have you ever been over here? On this side of town?"

"Not since I was a kid," Maggie said. "I think we called this 'The Bottoms' back then."

"We still call it that," Brett said. "At least at the police department."

He pulled to a stop in front of a one-story clapboard house. Maggie opened her car door and immediately wrinkled her nose from the stench of trash and ammonia. "Are you sure you don't want to come in?" She could hear several dogs in the distance, though it wasn't clear which house they belonged to.

"I think I should wait here, but whatever you do, don't go inside that house. Stay where I can see you."

Maggie agreed and left Brett in his car. As she and Ruby walked up the path to the house, they found themselves stepping carefully over large, broken cinder blocks, chunks of vehicle parts, and other things they couldn't make out in the dim glow of the front porch light.

She approached the front door with Ruby beside her. "Why don't you knock, Ruby? That way Daisy won't see me right away."

Ruby knocked hard on the door. "Hang on a minute," a voice called from inside. Maggie was sure that it belonged to Daisy.

They heard heavy footsteps approach the front door. A second later the door was yanked open, and a very large man stood looking down at them. "What do you want?"

The smell of ammonia nearly overwhelmed them as soon as the door was opened. Maggie cringed at the thought of Myra's wedding cakes being made inside the house.

"Are you John Michael?" Ruby asked in a voice Maggie didn't recognize. "I'm Ruby, a friend of a young girl who is in desperate need of her wedding cakes being ordered! Can you help me?"

The hulking man smiled grandly and called for Daisy over his shoulder. Maggie hung back in the shadows. "Sure, we can help," he said. "You just need to make sure that you can pay in full."

"We have cash," Maggie said. "She's already made a deposit."

"But we're prepared to pay a little extra if you need us to," Ruby said. Maggie smirked at Ruby's attempt to sound like a desperate woman.

"What is your friend's name?" Daisy asked when she crowded in the door frame with John Michael. She paused and stared hard at Maggie.

Out of the corner of her eye, Maggie noticed movement. She wasn't sure what she was looking at until Brooks and another officer stepped out of the shadows.

Daisy attempted to shut the door in Ruby's face.

John Michael, not clear about what was happening, blocked his wife from closing the door long enough for Brett to flash his badge and get a grip on him.

"Daisy McNorris, you are under arrest for trespassing," he said.

"Who do you think you are?" Daisy screamed when he pulled her out of the house and turned her around.

"Dogwood Mountain Chief of Police," he said.

"You, too, big guy," Brooks said. He pulled John Michael out of the doorway with the help of the other officer.

"What am I being charged with?" he asked. "You can't prove anything!"

"You're going to be charged with interfering with a police investigation, if you don't cooperate," Brooks said. "And for questioning in the same charges your wife is facing."

"And possibly more," Brett said. He walked Daisy down the road toward a pair of police cars Maggie didn't notice until then.

John Michael was placed in the back of one and Daisy in the other. Maggie followed Brett back to his car.

"I'm going to need the both of you to come down

to the station with me and give your statements about Daisy and her intrusion into Maggie's house," he said. "You two ride together and I'll fill you in after."

CHAPTER THIRTEEN

Maggie sat in the small waiting room outside of the administrative offices while Ruby gave her statement. She was still a little unsure about what was happening. She was hungry and tired and wanted to take the money in her pocket and throw it at the sheriff in Morton County and beg her to release Myra.

Brett appeared in the hallway a few minutes later. He carried two cans of coke and a bag of pretzels in his hand. "Your dinner, milady," he said when he slumped down in the chair beside her.

"You sure know how to treat a lady," Maggie said and plunged her hand into the bag of pretzels.

"Only the best for you, my dear," he said.

"Why are you smiling?" Maggie asked after she washed a mouthful of pretzels down with the coke.

"Because we got a confession," he said. "Two, in fact."

"You did?" She was suddenly very alert and on the edge of her seat. "I still have no idea how you guys even had enough to bring either of them in."

"Well, Theresa from the supply store played a big part. When you first talked to her, I think she was nervous, but I guess she saw you talking to Ruby, and since they are sort of familiar with each other, she felt compelled to help. She tracked down Brooks and told him basically the same thing that she told you, only Brooks went to a contact of his in Hunter Springs who was able to pull the phone records for the supply store."

"Theresa," Maggie said, surprised at the news. "So, how did Brooks know we were going to the house?"

"He didn't. He texted me as we pulled in and told me what he knew about the records. He said he was five minutes out with Officer Umbridge. He planned on bringing her in for questioning, but since she lives here in Dogwood Mountain, I was able to get involved."

"Wow. Talk about great timing."

"No kidding. And since we had proof it was Daisy who called her to change the number, all I had to do was bring her in for trespassing at your house and infer that I was suspicious of her for the murder of Wanda Reiss, and she sold her husband out."

"He killed Wanda?"

Brett nodded. "Turns out Wanda was his older sister and the two of them used to work in a bakery together near Tulsa. Wanda had a falling out with her family and moved away. When she wound up here, she tried to start her own business up. But she had no money to work with, so she started baking cakes out of her home."

"So, was John Michael her business partner or what?"

"He was just a former coworker at the family bakery. And he was fired at the same time Wanda left. Apparently, now this is from his confession, he was blamed for taking some money from the bakery and he blamed Wanda," Brett said.

"And they followed her here and basically did everything they could to make her life miserable?" Maggie said.

"Including usurping her efforts to start over again with wedding cakes," Brett said. "That's why Theresa had two numbers for the same person."

"Okay, then how did he end up killing her?" Maggie asked.

"According to Daisy, Wanda found out what they were up to, and she confronted John Michael at their home early the same morning she was supposed to meet up with Myra," Brett said. "They argued and he pushed her backward. She fell right there outside the front door and hit her head on one of those concrete blocks."

"But she was found way out on the highway close to the Morton County line," Maggie said.

"She was, and that's because John Michael put her body back in her car and drove all the way up there," Brett explained. "And Daisy showed up early to talk to Myra in order to throw off the timeline. That's why she showed up at your house, too."

"When she left, she made the drive up to Joplin to pick John Michael up, right?" The pieces began to fall together in Maggie's mind.

Brett nodded. "It was Daisy's idea to throw the blame toward Myra. She was just a convenience to them," he said. "They were convinced Wanda owed them all of the money she made and any business she found here."

"Is that why Daisy made that ridiculous demand for the money she said Myra still owed Wanda?"

"I think so," Brett said. "Either that or it was just

to make sure she made an impression on you. That way her alibi was more believable."

"But what about Wanda? Why did she demand a deposit from Myra and then back out of making her wedding cake?" Maggie asked.

"That part is a little fuzzy to me still, but I think when Wanda found out they had followed her here, Daisy tried to make nice and help Wanda out. I don't think the relationship lasted long, but that seems to be how she had access to Wanda's contacts here and her money," Brett said.

"She lied to Wanda and told her that Myra is the one who backed out," Brooks said from down the hall. He walked quickly toward them. "That part just came out. That's what started the falling out. Trust me, Chief. The longer you sit with those two, the more you find out about this entire mess."

"Where are you headed, Officer Macklin?" Brett asked.

"To Morton County to spring my wife-to-be out of jail," Brooks said with the biggest smile Maggie had ever seen on his face. "The sheriff just called. They have dropped the charges and plan to release her forthwith."

CHAPTER FOURTEEN

The sun shone brightly all day. The air was cool and crisp, but the sunshine made the day bright and festive. Maggie arrived early at the farm. She could smell the delicious aromas wafting from the kitchen before she walked through the back door.

Ruby's large kitchen buzzed with activity. Maggie shut the door behind her and waved to the two young assistants supplied by Ruby's editor and friend. Lindsey was the niece of her friend and Tony was her culinary classmate. Both had donned aprons and rolled up their sleeves early in the day.

"Hey, Maggie," Ruby called from her kitchen pantry. She emerged with a stack of seasonings in her arms.

"Are you going to have enough time?" Maggie asked.

"Enough time for what? To host a dinner reception and to shower and get ready for a wedding in a few hours? Oh, sure," Ruby said. She dumped the spices on the center island and collapsed into a chair at the table. "I am getting way too old to do this."

"I highly doubt that," Lindsey said. She picked up a half-dozen spice bottles and returned to the stove.

Within hours, the front field and the driveway were filled with cars. Maggie walked outside huddled in her winter coat and gazed at the barn, shining softly in the winter twilight.

"It's a little like a Thomas Kinkade painting, isn't it?" Brett stood next to her and wrapped one arm around her shoulder.

"I really can't believe how beautiful the old barn looks all lit up," she said. They walked together toward the barn and stood just outside.

When the cue was given, Brett released her shoulders and shucked off his outer coat. Maggie caught her breath when she saw him in his dress uniform and caught it again when she saw Brooks dressed the same. They began the procession, walking down the middle of the well-lit barn to the rustic pergola at the end.

Maggie shed her own coat and walked solo down the aisle, followed by Ruby, and stood under the lacy curtains. A moment later, the music changed and Orson, looking tall and regal, appeared at the barn entrance with Myra smiling on his arm. They walked slowly down the aisle. Maggie noticed the smile on Gretchen LeClair's face as they passed. Myra turned to face the minister after Orson kissed lightly on her forehead and then took his seat.

An hour later, Maggie sat on a hay bale alone with a champagne flute in her hand. Brett grinned at her from the other side of the barn and made his way toward her. His formal overcoat was gone. He approached her and took a seat on the hay bale beside her.

"I wondered where you were," he said. "Everything okay?"

Maggie nodded and sipped her champagne. "Everything is perfect. The ceremony was beautiful," she said.

"I came to tell you that Myra and Brooks are preparing to leave for their honeymoon," he said. "And they said that they have an announcement to make before they leave. I saw a large easel. I wonder what the announcement might be."

Maggie stood and took his arm. "You don't think

we're about to see a baby announcement, do you?" she asked as they walked toward the front of the barn.

"I can tell you a young police officer who will never hear the end of it if that is the case," Brett said.

Myra and Brooks stood on either side of the easel, grinning eagerly. Myra had changed out of her beautiful wedding dress and into a subtle off-white pants suit for their flight to California.

"Everyone, if we could have your attention," Brooks called out. He beamed at his bride as he spoke. "We have been working on a huge project behind the scenes. And even with the unfortunate events of the past few days, we were able to complete this little project just in time."

"Someone remind me never to order another cake from a stranger," Myra said. Laughter roared through the barn. "All joking aside, we are so excited to be able to share this with our loved ones."

"Before we pull off the cover and reveal the big secret, we need some help from a dear friend. Orson, would you join us down here?" he asked.

Orson's head bobbed up. He looked around at the crowd, clearly confused. "Me? You need help from me?"

"Just get over here, please," Myra said.

"Yes, Ma'am," Orson said. He blushed slightly as he walked toward the front. He stood next to Myra under the pergola. Brooks stood on the other side of the easel. He clutched the bottom of the white towel in his hand.

"When I asked Myra to marry me, we agreed on one thing," he began. "Well, we agreed on a number of things, but a big one was the desire to remain in this area for the rest of our lives. We plan to raise our family here."

"Someday," Myra interjected. "Let's be clear. No babies today. Someday, but not today."

"Anyway, we started our search right away and quickly found a new home on the outskirts of Dogwood Mountain," Brooks said. He yanked the towel off of the easel and revealed an extra-large photo of a tall, three-story house.

"That's the old O'Donnell place," Brett said.

"It is," Myra said. Maggie felt the ache in her heart watching her young friend grinning with so much happiness. Brett appeared to think the same thoughts. He pulled her close to him and whispered in her ear.

"I'm so glad she is here and able to enjoy all of this," he said.

Maggie rested her head on his chest and blinked back the tears.

"You have a new house?" Angeline Macklin, Brooks's doting aunt, shouted, and clapped from the middle of the crowd.

"We do, and we have spent many long days remodeling it from the inside out," Brooks announced. "We still have quite a bit of work to do, but we've already come so far."

"As you can see, this is a huge house," Myra said. "The main house has five bedrooms and three bathrooms."

"But as you can see, there is an addition on the back of the house at the ground level," Brooks continued.

"Many years ago, the O'Donnell family added a mother-in-law suite on the back behind the kitchen."

"That's where you come in, Orson." Myra smiled. "The suite has a small bedroom, bathroom, and a sitting room that opens up to the kitchen."

Orson shook his head. "I'm afraid I don't understand any of this," he said.

"We're asking for you to come and stay with us, instead of me staying with you, old man," Myra said.

She hooked her arm through his, as she had done

when they walked down the aisle a couple of hours before.

"What? You want me to live with you?" Orson asked.

"Let me make this a little easier," Brooks said. "Not that I am itching to get my bride on a plane or anything." The crowd laughed heartily at his comment. "Orson, you opened your home up to my wife when she was homeless and scared. You, along with Maggie and Ruby, rescued her and gave her a second chance at a good life. I don't know if it has occurred to you pal, but she loves you like a father."

"And when we looked at this house, we both had the same thought at the exact same time," Myra cut in. Her voice broke with emotion. "We both decided that this addition on the back would be the perfect place for you to spend the rest of your days in peace and comfort. That old house of yours is getting to be a lot to keep up with."

"So, what do you say, old man? Are you up for some new digs? I can guarantee the heat and air work," Brooks said. He stepped forward and held out a set of keys to Orson. "Thanks to Jake and Flo, your room and furniture are already set up. All you have to do is go home."

Tears ran down Orson's face. He stepped forward

and took the keys from Brooks, then caught both bride and groom up in an epic hug.

***

If you enjoyed Cake It To Heart, check out the next book in the series, The Hole Truth, today!

AUTHOR'S NOTE

I'd love to hear your thoughts on my books, the storylines, and anything else that you'd like to comment on—reader feedback is very important to me. My contact information, along with some other helpful links, is listed on the next page. If you'd like to be on my list of "folks to contact" with updates, release and sales notifications, etc.… just shoot me an email and let me know. Thanks for reading!

Also…

… if you're looking for more great reads, Summer Prescott Books publishes several popular series by outstanding Cozy Mystery authors.

CONTACT SUMMER PRESCOTT BOOKS PUBLISHING

Blog and Book Catalog: http://summerprescottbooks.com

Email: summer.prescott.cozies@gmail.com

And…be sure to check out the Summer Prescott Cozy Mysteries fan page and Summer Prescott Books Publishing Page on Facebook – let's be friends!

To sign up for our fun and exciting newsletter, which will give you opportunities to win prizes and swag, enter contests, and be the first to know about New Releases, click here: http://summerprescottbooks.com